PRAISE FOR SIGF
HISTOR

C000170749

"A complex and arresting n
an ingenious constr
—Nomination Committee for the Women's Literature Prize

"As her state of mind becomes increasingly fraught, Lytton
Smith's adept translation skillfully conveys [the narrator's] neurotic,
internal experience, which often expresses possibilities, thoughts,
speculation, and interpretations instead of an external reality."
—Callum McAllister, *Asymptote Journal*

"*History. A Mess.* . . . is at once a disturbing but riveting portrait
of a glassy psyche and an enlightening critique of the constraints and
pressures of modern scholarship." —Bailey Trela, *Ploughshares*

"Fans of the nouveau roman—Marguerite Duras, Alain Robbe-
Grillet, Nathalie Sarraute, etc.—will be right at home here."
—*Kirkus Reviews*

"Pálsdóttir writes with the hand of a mystery author and the
mind of a postmodernist, teasing out her protagonist's problem while
playing with literary forms, fragmenting timelines, and injecting
fierce irony."—*Publishers Weekly*

"What I admire most about Pálsdóttir's writing is her ability to
hide a strictly structured course of events under a gliding, occasion-
ally deliberately (but not distractingly) chaotic style; her ability to or-
chestrate the random; to construct a perspective for the narrator that,
most of the time, reveals both everything and nothing about what is
actually going on; and the way she covers real tensions and worries
with a quilt of details, as they are so often covered in life."
—Rein Raud, *European Literature Network*

ALSO IN ENGLISH BY
SIGRÚN PÁLSDÓTTIR

History. A Mess.

EMBROIDERY

SIGRÚN PÁLSDÓTTIR

TRANSLATED BY LYTTON SMITH

OPEN LETTER

LITERARY TRANSLATIONS FROM THE UNIVERSITY OF ROCHESTER

Originally published in Icelandic as *Delluferðin* by Forlagið
Copyright © Sigrún Pálsdóttir, 2019
Translation copyright © Lytton Smith, 2023

Library of Congress Cataloging-in-Publication data: Available.

ISBN (pb): 978-1-948830-76-8 | ISBN (ebook) 978-1-948830-89-8

Cover design by Anna Jordan

Published by Open Letter at the University of Rochester
Dewey Hall 1-219, RC Box 278968, Rochester, NY 14627
www.openletterbooks.org

EMBROIDERY

The noise came from downstairs. A strange murmur of human voices. For a moment, I was sure I was dreaming, because I couldn't make out what was being said. Then I heard my grandmother's low snoring beside me. That told me I was awake. I got out of bed, crawling over her tiny body, and snuck along the loft to lie on the floor with my face jutting out part way into the opening at the top of the stairs.

Through the tobacco smoke that filled the living room, I could see an elderly man sitting on the couch next to a younger woman. The man was wearing a brown jacket and a blue cravat; the woman was wearing a green overcoat and, underneath it, a blouse with ivory lace around her neck. Old Magnús was sitting opposite these two; Guðlaug stood by the coffee pot, pouring a cup. Dad was in the chair under the window and my mother was sitting on the chest alongside it, a little ways off from the smoke and the man's monologue, which ended with the young woman in lace saying something and then pointing at her coffee cup. She seemed to be directing her words to my mom, who kept smiling and nodding in a way I didn't recognize. In fact, I found my mother's appearance somehow peculiar, her back unusually bowed as she sat against the living room wall. But then she sat up straighter as Dad said a few words I knew were in answer to the foreign woman's questions. After he'd spoken, the two visitors stood to leave, with Magnús and Dad following them out. It was then that I got a better look at the woman's outfit, her voluminous skirt spilling away from her tiny waist and swaying in all directions as she glided across the living room floor. I crept back along the floor, climbed over Grandma again, and appeared fast asleep by the time mom stroked my cheek. She gently rested her index finger on the tip of my nose. She could tell I was awake.

The next morning, no one mentioned the evening visit, and I didn't ask. I didn't ask because I didn't need to know anything. The memory of that alien scent was enough for me, the image of the people, the way the visit had somehow enlarged our little living room since that night. Still, it wasn't as if I spent all my time thinking about the glamorous strangers; in fact, I'd almost forgotten their visit until, one summer day, I was helping my mom with the housework and caught sight of a colorful little picture lying on a stack of papers on my dad's desk. It was on top of some unopened envelopes. A postcard. I put down my cleaning cloth and held the picture in front of me with two hands:

Somewhere, in a big city, getting toward dusk, magnificently-sized snowflakes were falling to earth, glinting light across the scene. A little girl was pulling her mother toward a shop window so she could show her a large reindeer. A man with a black top hat, wearing a fur-collared coat, held a large package as he led his wife along. In their wake, a young man dragged a large Christmas tree behind him, while on the other side of the street, boys were making snowballs to throw at the gleaming black horse-drawn carriage passing by. Everyone was engaged in some activity but had been frozen mid-action. Everyone except the young woman in the right corner of the picture. She seemed to have been standing still before the moment struck, and there was no way to know whether she was heading across the street or along it. She was wearing a dark blue coat and had a little red hat on her head; her hands inside a brown faux muff clutched tight to her stomach. Her face was much clearer than the others on the postcard; she looked bewildered.

I was wondering if she was by herself when I realized Mom was standing behind me. She bent down, resting her chin on my shoulder. Out of the corner of my eye, I saw her smile when she said that this Christmas card was a little late on its travels. Then she straightened up and continued cleaning. I turned the card over. It was addressed to Brand Johnson but in the top corner was the sender's address: New York, December 15, 1879. The writing was difficult to read and messy and of course I didn't understand any of it. But I felt like I knew where the card had come from.

Later that same day, after a little pestering, my father let me keep the postcard. I put it in the little chest I kept by my feet, so I could retrieve it when I had trouble falling asleep after the family reading. And no matter how dark the black got that winter of 1880, I could always see the picture if I held the card in front of me long enough. In the darkness, I actually saw something I hadn't noticed before: in a narrow, snow-packed side street, two well-dressed men were facing each other, deep in conversation. As I kept looking, though, I felt as if their attention was really on the young woman in the red hat with the muff. I came to feel that the despair in her face must stem from knowing that they were watching her—that she was trying to make up her mind about what she should do if the frozen moment would suddenly come to an end.

I felt my hand fall. The postcard dropped down onto my blanket and at the same moment the young woman with the red *hat ran across the street, through the large and ornate letters in the right corner of the picture, A MERRY CHRISTMAS, and from there out of the frame. Simultaneously, the men were set in motion, heading the same way. They didn't run but walked confidently across the street, taking long strides, easily clearing through the Christmas greeting, already gone by the time I heard a creak on the stairs. I flinched, and in my half-conscious state it seemed that my grandmother was coming hobbling along the floor to our bed. I lay there, eyes closed, fumbling for the postcard, which I gently snuck under the blanket. Grandma leaned in, but I turned to the other side. And before her rattling locked me inside the narrow world of our loft, I myself was dashed into the dark alley, floating over the snowdrifts in my white nightgown, there behind the two men and the young woman they were pursuing.*

I

A symposium in Reykjavík, March 1897.
The evening draws to a close.

"And it's this very belt tip she intended to buy for nearly fifteen thousand dollars. From the owner, a young Icelandic woman by the name of Branson. Miss Selena Branson." The Governor rises from his seat. He walks over to the living room window and watches the snowflakes hanging in the air, the light of the white square, Lækjartorg, illuminating the black darkness: "So, I ask you, my dear friends, if this Branson woman isn't in fact Sigurlína Brandsdóttir, daughter of Brandur Jónson, the scholar and scribe from Kot in Skagafjörður."

The proof in the pudding! Catching the Governor's guests completely off guard. The Chief Justice howls: "Rubbish!" The Priest wailed: "Oh, no!" The District Commissioner bursts out: "Brand's pawn?" The Poet smirks: "Little pawn!" The Historian cries, "Pawn?" The Treasurer marvels: "Fifteen thousand dollars? How can one small, old object be so valuable? Isn't that tantamount to the Icelandic National Bank's entire savings?"

But the seventh guest, the handsome young Editor, shows no reaction as he sits slightly apart from the other men, almost up against the wall. He leans forward, his eyes fixed on the small stain on the oriental rug, a hand-woven carpet that covers the floor of this opulent old room. He's trying to call to mind a girl's face, but he can't see anything except a thin white gown around a small body, a gilded belt cinched at her waist, a pretty bosom covered with thin light-colored strands of hair, an edged collar colored with golden embroidery, a Greek pattern. Around her neck, a black ribbon; on her head, a golden tiara. And then, finally, he conjures up her face. First, thin lips which smile, snigger, under a fine nose, a little upturned; the nostrils flare as if the girl tries to hold back her laughter, hold back her strength and character. Her eyes are hidden behind a black ball mask. But he can still see them. Aqua under heavy eyelids framed from below by thin, stiff bags. A bewitching glance that drives him crazy, thrills him so that he startles and whispers the name aloud to himself, "Sigurlína," then raises his head to see that they are looking at him inquiringly: Governor, Chief Justice, Priest, District Commissioner, Poet, Historian, Treasurer. Is he supposed to say something?

The young man leans back, against the thick stone wall of this low-ceilinged living room—this former prison, a hovel, as some call this official residence. Leaning back, he almost disappears behind an ailing tropical plant that's standing alongside the wall right next to the white-painted frame around the door out of the room. And there, behind the door, is the maid. Eavesdropping. She's a tall, buxom woman, and she has her ear right up to the door. In one hand, she holds an empty crystal carafe; her other hand flies to her mouth. But when none of the Governor's guests seems inclined to react any further to the question he's posed and the information he's revealed, the woman retreats cautiously but purposefully from the door. She walks briskly down the hallway, unopposed, and heads into the kitchen. She sets down the bottle then tidies away her apron and takes off the cap. By the back door she puts on her coat, buttons it, and wraps a shawl around her shoulders. She opens the door. A snowdrift has formed a wall in the doorway that reaches her thighs, but little matter, because she pushes her way out and through with such force that the newly fallen snow whirls up before her. She struggles in the direction of the stone wall that surrounds the house and swings herself deftly over it.

The woman takes short strides, having to lift her legs quite high, going down Bankastræti; when she turns onto Austurstræti and is passing by the Treasurer's house, she almost loses her balance. A cry escapes her lips, only a small one, but in the cold stillness of Reykjavík, it's loud enough to startle a young maiden and drive a sewing needle into the tip of finger as she sits in her best chair by her living room window, embroidering embossed gold onto green slippers. The young woman rises from her chair and brings a small oil lamp up to the windowsill. She presses her fair face against the window and takes the bleeding finger out of her mouth: "There's hardly call to hurry," though by then the Governor's fast-moving servant has already disappeared from sight, heading west. And she continues with great purpose, steadily increasing her speed. Then, when she reaches the corner of Aðalstræti, she stumbles upon two crazy, rearing horses, and falls face forward down in the snow. An old woman, a water bearer, standing stock still in the snow in front of Hotel

Iceland, sighs some rough, incoherent words into the air but then moves toward the woman, reaching out her swollen, blue hand. The maid waves her away and gets to her feet without assistance. She shakes off the snow as she continues her journey, now taking larger strides than before, almost running, finally even crawling through the snow. It's clear she has no time to lose. She needs to get to Brandur's house right away, while the story of Selena Branson, little Lína, with all its digressions, gaps and wonders, is still clear in her head.

A Picnic. Late Summer, 1896.

Early in the morning, there was a knock on the door of Brandur's house. Silvía Popp was standing outside, desperate. Flapping her arms all around in anguish. She needed help with a lunch basket. The picnic was for some Americans who were going to ride out of town with her father, up to the valley, Elliðaárdalur, leaving in half an hour; Sussí Thordarsen had cancelled at the last minute. Time was running away, so Silvía took Lína's broad smile as an agreement, then rushed off toward town. Sigurlína went outside and watched her friend run down the road, waving eagerly after her even though she knew Silvía couldn't see her. She closed the door and leaned back against it, a smile still on her face. Then she jumped up and was about to get dressed but stopped at the living room door, turned around and looked down at the kitchen table. The legs of lamb Guðmundur had brought were still lying there. "The devil with it!" she whispered, softly, throwing the shanks into the pantry and remembering everything else she hadn't taken care of. Dirty laundry, ribbons to embroider for Þórdís, the entire kitchen floor, a pile of papers on her father's desk, including two English letters she had to copy out, due tomorrow. They would have to wait, she thought; she was heading out. Out of town to meet strangers.

About fifteen minutes later, she was standing in her riding clothes in her father's office with a small, folded slip of paper in her palm. She set it on the table, pushed the thought of her father's reaction away, thinking instead of her mother, how it was the anniversary of her death. She left the house and followed the route into town, almost at a run by the time she reached Aðalstræti. A vagrant drunk hollered at her—what, she couldn't possibly tell, and she didn't care a jot because at that same moment she saw Jón Jónsson, the Editor, walking along Austurstræti, heading west. So beautiful and so deep in thought. She wondered where he was coming from this early; she kept to her side of the street, looking down when they met, not wanting him to know where she was going.

When she turned off Austurstræti, she saw two men outside the merchant's house. They were saddling the horses while Silvía and her father stood by. Soon, three large and handsome men arrived, and after that, two young women joined the group. These were beautiful women, wearing domed hats and close-cut jackets over substantial dresses. Sigurlína stroked her riding habit and now felt them lacking, made of poor material, too stiff and wide. Like a cylinder around her slender, scrawny body. But she didn't have much time to think about it, because Popp was already giving orders left and right and beginning to arrange the horses. The people mounted and shortly the army rode out into the square, across the bridge and east, accompanied by shouts and questions from the Americans to Popp and little Pétur, the assistant, about anything they saw going on as they made their way out of town. The one who talked most was Mr. Watson, an American businessman and the group's leader; the owner of the ship that had brought the people to Iceland was Mr. Wilson, friendly in appearance and middle-aged like Watson, his partner. The third man, Mr. Johnson, was considerably younger. He seemed hardly there at all. One of the women was Mrs. Wilson, the other Miss Baker. Sigurlína knew nothing about how these people were connected to one another.

The Americans took the lead. Through the cloud of dust, she looked at the backs of the two women, the exotic hats on their heads and the shoulder padding on the jackets so puffy that the women's waistlines seemed strangely narrow. As the group headed out of town, Sigurlína passed the time by cutting herself a new riding habit out of velvet and wool.

From the hilltop at Skólavörðuholt, the route passed through Öskjuhlíð and from there north along Bústaðaholt. As the group approached their destination, it was getting warmer, and the sun had risen high by the time they stopped near the waterfall, Kermóafoss. The foreigners inspected their surroundings, but Sigurlína and Silvía immediately started to get things out of the chest. They laid a white cloth on the ground, made the coffee, and arranged the food on the cloth: bread, cakes, and some meat. Sausage rolls. The American women sat down on the ground, picked up the food like little birds under their parasols. Soon the two were walking up the river. The three men shortly went off with Popp and Pétur.

After they had cleaned up from lunch, Silvía went to join the group, but Sigurlína sat down on a tussock above the grassy plain and picked up her stuff. The ribbons for Þórdís. The golden wire glistened beautifully in the scorching sun, but the heat under the skirts was so uncomfortable that she almost wanted to twist them up. But suddenly she was in shadow. Some big, white toes in the grass before her: "Sæll vertú!" said a deep voice, followed by a belly laugh. She looked up. In front of her stood the man who had taken the lead on the way up. Mr. Watson, tall and broad, with a large beard and dark hair. Not unattractive. Come to this country, according to his own words, to have fun with a group of good friends. He crouched down and for a moment came awkwardly close to her as he stroked a large, coarse index finger over the goldwork flowers on the black velvet ribbon and whispered, "Treasure. For sale?" But before Sigurlína could answer the man's question, he suddenly got up, stroked his beard and looked at the sky: "The western world is obsessed with ancient ruins and artifacts. And has been for a long time now." Then he took a tiny step to one side and lay flat on the grass with his hands under his neck. He took a deep breath: "Museums and collectors' cabinets are filled with classical remains, Roman and Greek marbles of all shapes and sizes, vases and bowls and statues." Watson raised his other hand and stuck out his index finger: "But as these remains continue to prevail all around us, they will eventually give rise to interest in other cultures, more remote and peculiar. Like Icelandic culture!"

Sigurlína didn't quite know how to react to the man's lofty statements, but before she could put a few general words together into too small an answer, the people began to gather back in the field. The youngest in the group, Mr. Johnson, walked, giggling, over to Watson, nudging his shoulder with one of his feet. Watson pretended to be asleep.

The journey back went smoothly, and when Watson dismounted in front of the merchant's house in the square at Lækjartorg, he announced to Sigurlína and that he would come to her house tomorrow to buy needlework and Icelandic things.

She'd achieved her goal for the excursion. In the twilight on the way home, she enumerated her trunk's contents: embroidered ribbons, two promised to Þórdís and almost ready; tablecloths, pillows, sofa cushions, old needle roll. Wool socks? Yes, Watson had mentioned them, she had understood that much. And she also had plenty of mittens. It was a little better selling those to foreigners than sitting incessantly knitting for townspeople. What else? she thought, as she headed inside. From the kitchen she went to the living room. From there she saw her father through the slit, inside his office. She withdrew. He knew she was there but didn't look up. And he heard her as she went upstairs. An eternal, distant presence.

She immediately started rummaging in her stuff, digging in the trunk, shaking the dust off, smoothing out, patting and stroking. Then she went to bed and with her eyes closed pictured how she would lay her things out on the table in the living room as soon her father had gone to the Antiquarian Collection of Iceland, on the top floor of the Alþingishúsið, the Icelandic parliament, where he would sit amid his findings and record the items that came to the collection and try to have them displayed for tourists. She reached for her book but struggled to concentrate. Noises came through the window. Sounds of drinking and fighting from next door.

The old couple scuffling. Not so long ago the woman had practically bitten the man's finger off, but now it was like she was underneath him, wailing. Sigurlína covered her ears and looked at the picture of her mother hanging on the wall by the bed; her set face, its innate gentleness.

Suddenly everything became quiet. As if she had been transferred to the time in her life when the face in the frame had filled her world. A few images came to mind: outside, by the storehouse, covering her ears when her brother was born; under a blanket with Mom reading folktales; sewing with her, too, a little dress for a doll, and learning to write; baking cakes in the dark; looking at a Christmas postcard from overseas in mid-summer; playing Slapjack with Grandma; Grandma dead beside her in her bed; a man under a black cloth, an explosion, blazing light, she didn't dare stir, didn't dare step away from where she was standing in front of the white sheet that hung over the farm door; letting herself dream of the future that began with a long journey south to Reykjavík in 1884 at the age of fourteen. A single uninterrupted image of riding away from her childhood, away from their farm in the valley, over the current-swollen waters of Héraðsvötn and to Víðimýri where her mother lay sick for a few days, a child in her womb. To Bólstaðarhlíð next and finally Gilshagi in Vatnsdalur before they set up on Grímstunguheiði. They set up their tent by Lake Arnarvatn and at sunrise she awoke to birdsong. The two of them carefully crawled out of the tent and walked down to the lake. What had her mother been saying to her? Sigurlína couldn't remember, only that it was awfully quiet. And she felt as if she were going to die there amid all this silence, because in the mirror-smooth water, in her mother's sweet smile, she sensed suffering and fear.

Until a flat stone bounced along the surface of the water. Her father and brother had got to their feet. Everyday life had been awakened and with it the pain eased. And under the safe guidance of her father, the four of them headed for their next destination, Kalmanstunga.

As elsewhere, they were well received; every farmer knew her father. They spent that night at the farm, her mother getting good rest in the housewife's big bed before the trip across Kaldadalur valley the next day. That was a long stretch, because even though the sun warmed the air between the glaciers, the road was difficult and they often had to dismount and lead the horses by the reins over the most snow-covered parts. Eventually this image appeared, almost like the one in the frame above their sofa, the watercolor picture of grassy green fields by the lake Þingvallavatn.

They rode through town late at night. Along the streets, past houses she had only ever seen in photographs. They headed straight for the house her father had bought for them the past spring. Sigurlína thought it was rather small and felt more cramped than their old farm in the north, even though the house was practically empty; their belongings had not yet arrived, so they had to sleep on the floor that first night, with blankets and other things under them. Another night, too—the night her mother gave birth to her baby. Sigurlína slept, but when she woke up her mother and the child had been taken away. A boy she never saw because he was immediately taken into foster care after it became clear that her mother would not return.

Sigurlína was standing inside the empty living room. There were two women with her father. He hugged her tightly, kissed her on her head. One of the women stroked her hair. She couldn't remember anything more until that evening. Then their father walked with his two children down into town, to the main street. At the end of it stood the hospital. They went up to the second floor. She heard noises inside the building but didn't know where the sounds were coming from. "And now I must bid you farewell," said a male voice. "What? You're leaving? No, you're not allowed to, it's impossible!" replied another. When they reached the upper floor, she could no longer hear the words. Their path lay along a dark corridor. Into a small room. Her mother lying there. "We haven't gotten to the bottom of this matter with the huckleberries!" Huckleberries? And now Sigurlína realized the words were resounding from the ground floor of the building. Her father didn't react to the noises but gently pushed Sigurlína toward the bed. She put her hand on her mother's head and leaned forward. She kissed her forehead. Rock hard and cold under her silky skin. "Bravo! I'm in the mood! And if there's something you want—I suspect there may be several things—come straight to me." Now her father shook his head in displeasure, leading his son to the bed. "Childhood is like a hike!" And then they were on their way out. They walked down the stairs to cheers and applause. Doors opened and theater guests burst out of the auditorium.

A strange existence began, an existence without emotion, a scenario in fog. The little boy, her youngest brother, died shortly afterward. But somehow the house filled up with furniture and belongings. Somehow she entered the kitchen, was standing there at the stove stirring a pot. Somehow the three of them sat down and ate. And somehow she mastered the feeling awakened by seeing her father and brother without her mother—that feeling of not actually existing but still acutely sensing the great pain this infinite, corrosive emptiness aroused. She had entered a whole new world in Reykjavík, yet felt her perception had been halved; until now she had looked at the world with her mother by her side.

No one was mean to her, though, and surely she loved her distant father and her brother too, although he seemed to be drifting into a different world than the one she was living in. And they didn't exactly want for anything, because her father immersed himself in work and soon the authorities had given him the provisional appointment with the Antiquarian Collection. But she couldn't be sure that her life was going to be what she had previously expected, the future her mother had promised her shortly before her Confirmation. In fact, it wasn't until after the third winter in Reykjavík that Sigurlína carefully brought up the Reykjavík Women's Gymnasium school to her father, and did so again around the time her brother took his entrance exam to the Reykjavík Junior College. On both occasions she didn't dare mention her mother's promise for fear of upsetting him. Her father shook his head, saying something about this desire for education being senseless and that she already knew everything they taught there, in that mess, which is how he referred to school—and when she talked about the English she wanted to learn, he said he couldn't spare her from duties at home right now, though he half-promised her something for the future, only to take those words back right away, saying that her work copying from the dictionary and all the translations he worked on with her help would teach her more Anglo-Saxon than Mrs. Sigríður ever could. Then he handed her two English novels and told her that if she got through these, she would have no need to attend school.

But what Brandur didn't understand was that his daughter first and foremost longed to get out of the house a little more often. She had her girlfriends, of course, and sometimes she also went down Aðalstræti to the Editor's house to teach the couple's youngest daughter needlework. It did her good to go there. The lady's presence reminded her of her mother's warm welcome, and sometimes Jón Jr's friends were sitting in the kitchen. She enjoyed hearing them converse; she felt alive even though it was often empty tomfoolery and nonsense, especially when the old Editor, the father of the family, wasn't around. But the best of all was being near Jón, even though proximity to him made her increasingly confused and insecure. He had a tendency to look away when they talked, but he always looked into her eyes when he asked what she was reading, what she was working on with her father.

She saw that the picture of her mother hung slightly askew on the wall. She stretched out her hand to straighten it out. She closed her eyes, took a deep breath, and turned to the side. At the same moment, the frame swung back the same way.

*Watson held the cylinder, brought it up to one eye as if
it were a telescope*

When Sigurlína came down in the morning, her father had gone to work. She carried her stuff down and laid it on the living room table. Then she went into the pantry to find something for the guests and saw where the legs of lamb were lying on the table. She was half-expecting Watson and his party at any moment but knew that the meat couldn't wait much longer. She was of two minds, but she put on her apron and started to clean the meat and cut it into pieces. After that, she resolutely went to work. Got sugar, salt and saltpeter, and got all messy. Went into the pantry and grabbed the barrel. She heard people talking outside and jumped, only to find it was just some cottagers. She salted the bottom of the barrel and began to tread. Poured water, salted, stuffed, and pressed until the meat was tenderized. Then she put the lid on the barrel, pushed it down, and put the weight on top. She put the barrel back, swept the kitchen floor and scrubbed. She looked around, thinking how unfortunate it was that they didn't have a front entrance, that they had to let people in the house through the kitchen all the time. Degrading, especially when newcomers and foreigners came to visit.

Now she tidied away her apron, ran upstairs, and changed into something nicer. Then back down to the kitchen to prepare coffee. She had nothing but a single soda cake and a few donuts to serve. That would have to do. She took out the coffee set and laid it on the table. She rearranged her things, a few pairs of brown half socks and some calf socks and mittens, one pair embroidered. She smoothed the cross-stitched tablecloth, the two black wool pads, the floral pattern cushion. She adjusted how the cuffs were arranged on the table, the embroidered ribbons, the needle roll, and a very old collar. Not bad at all, she thought, and sat down on the living room sofa and began to wait for the people to come. Read again about earthquakes in the newspaper but with her mind on something else, looking out the window, going upstairs to pick up a novel and to look in the mirror, going into the pantry and back out to the window, sitting on the couch again, looking out into the air, thinking all sorts of thoughts until she fell asleep on the couch and dreamed she was far out of town, where the ground was shaking and people were running naked out of buildings that were falling to the ground with a loud bang that caused her to jump up. A knock at the door.

The guests drank coffee and chatted. Sigurlína answered their questions and their conversation flowed for a while. Then they finally rose and went over to the table. Watson was unusually silent but Mrs. Wilson complimented the tablecloth as she gently pulled it up from the table. Miss Baker grabbed the collar, set it around her neck, and adopted a strange expression; Watson picked up a pair of low socks and said they would buy everything on the table. He handed Sigurlína a bundle of banknotes. While the women packed up the stuff in their baskets, Watson walked around the living room, reached out to the wall shelf, and picked up her mother's old tail cap tassel cylinder. Watson held the cylinder, brought it up to one eye as if it were a telescope. Then he realized. Sigurlína, still holding the notes from him in her hand, approved of his discovery by nodding her head, and they both laughed as he held it vertically up to his temple. Then he asked if the silver object was for sale. Sigurlína didn't dare answer. She didn't know what to answer. Watson carefully put the cylinder back on the shelf.

After the people left the house, she stood in the kitchen, still, thinking odd thoughts. She rubbed the notes and counted them, brought them to her nose and sniffed. Her hands smelled of brine. She ran upstairs, put the money in her chest, and rejoiced. Then she flew back down again because now she had plenty to do. She put the pot of water over the fire and started cutting the rhubarb stalks into small pieces, slowly, while she watched poor old Álfrún out in the garden. She stood there, bowed low among the hens, trying to get some morsels from off the ground—an image so familiar that Sigurlína almost felt as if it were a picture painted on the glass. Out on the low, flat rock, shouts could be heard from some children who seemed to be heading for the sandy shore.

Clasp

Watson and his friends had gone to Geysir. It rained a lot in Reykjavík the next few days, and Sigurlína was mostly alone at home working, her brother still up north. He had gone there after his final exams to work for the district commissioner. His future was uncertain; Brandur had asked him to postpone his trip to Copenhagen in the autumn to allow some anticipated money to come in. Sigurlína and her father worked on the dictionary and translations, but he was also engaged in sundry kinds of scribing and had promised some people a copy of the *Vínland Sagas*, a job he would hand on to her when he was completely snowed under. And days went by, one after another, until one day the sun finally showed itself and Brandur asked his daughter to come down to the museum after her housework was done. He needed a little help with some of the artifacts he had received a few days ago.

Was she forgetting anything? Sigurlína stood vacillating in the doorway around noon, having made their three beds, swept the bedroom floors, repaired their socks, made bread dough, rubbed and soaked the cheese, washed the dripping linen, wrung it and spread it out under the morning sun, sorted the dirty laundry and set it to soak—her father's underwear separately—soaked the almonds, soaked prunes and raisins, soaked fish, soaked cabbage, soaked everything that could be soaked in this little house, soaked, finally, her own soaked-through hands, her crumpled little fingertips, in warm, soapy water. No, that was all, she thought, and slammed the door behind her, running off; she had made it to Austurvöllur Square by the time she remembered two loose buttons on her father's vest.

She walked wearily into the Parliament house and straight up to the second floor. She heard voices from inside the workshop. She immediately realized that the Poet was there, but when she entered she saw that they were three sitting at her father's table. One of them was Dr. Finnsson, the young scholar from England, who had come to find Brandur last night. "Affectatious" was the word her father had used to describe the young man. The third man, she had never seen before.

When Brandur saw his daughter approaching, he raised his hand in the air to signal that she should wait. She took a few steps back, went into the hall, leaned against the wall, up by the old chasuble, her hands behind her back, and gasped. She looked down at the sole of her shoe, which seemed to be coming off the tip of her toe, and listened to the men talking on the other side of the wall. She felt some agitation in the air. They talked about some "he" who did not have the power to stop some "it," and how her father had to go north as soon as possible. Then something was said in English, and after that it was as if a settlement had been reached at the table, because now the men lowered their voices and spoke intermittently as if their communication no longer required words. But Sigurlína had grown rather tired of standing up there, so she leaned forward on the display case, her elbows on the glass, looking over all sorts of things from antiquity; that old wretched mitten. And there she stood for a few minutes or so until she gave up and felt she needed to take a seat. She knew very well that she wasn't allowed to sit in the knight's throne, but it was either the ancient chair or the floor. She sat up straight with her hands on the knights' arms, itching her palms by stroking their fractures, and she was recalling how they had broken when the Poet suddenly came walking into the hall. Sigurlína sprang up from the chair. After him came Finnsson, in that bulky trench coat with his gloved hands, swinging a walking stick, and then the elegant third man. And as the trio left the hall, the stranger turned around, looking in Sigurlína's direction. It all happened in an instant; she couldn't make out his face distinctly. She could certainly see, however, that he had winked one eye at her.

Her father was in his workshop, surrounded by all sorts of rubbish. He told her to pick up a rag and start wiping things down with it. There were human bone parts, a lone arrowhead, all sorts of rusty fragments of various things she couldn't quite identify. But it wasn't all junk: there was a large sword, a comb made of bone, and a tongue-shaped object that fit snugly in her palm. She gently rubbed her cloth over this little brass shield; in places, it seemed to have a golden sheen. She looked at the shield, at the pattern on the front. An engraving, something like a string, coiled around inside the frame. She went over to the window and let the midday sun's rays fall on the object. Now she saw that the string was a worm, or perhaps some kind of dragon with a narrow body and long tail. "A cape clasp," Brandur whispered without looking up from his work. She turned the object around and saw that at the top of the shield, the foil, was a small pin; at the bottom was a loop. The needle itself was missing. She looked in the windowpane and held the clasp up between her breasts, pretending to be an Icelandic settler woman, then suddenly lost sight of her own reflection as she saw Jón walking along Kirkjustræti. With a lady. She moved closer to the glass, but before she could figure out who the woman was, her father made a sound that sent her back to her seat.

Brandur had completed the inventory and now Sigurlína had to neatly copy out his report regarding the artifacts. About the cape clasp she wrote, following her father, *Tongue-shaped brooch, made of bronze, from around 1000. Probably from a pair. Almost intact and undamaged and very well fashioned. A rare item.* Then she noted the size of the brooch and his detailed description of the pattern that confirmed its age. Next, the bones. A jawbone and several molars.

Brandur decided to stay a while longer but Sigurlína set off for home. On the way, she stopped by the Editor's house to pick up a piece of fabric the lady of the house had promised her. People were sitting in the living room: Jón the younger, the future editor, with a young woman next to him on the sofa. A woman Sigurlína didn't know. Probably the one she had just seen through the Parliament building's window. The woman looked a little older than Sigurlína. Older than Jón. She introduced herself in Danish. The lady handed the material to Sigurlína and smiled at her in a way she understood to be compassion. Her smile was tender and pitying.

Sigurlína went out on Aðalstræti and turned west. Who was the Danish woman? For a moment, she was a bit upset, but then she thought that if things were as she suspected, then no matter; she was entirely indifferent. And suddenly, she felt excitement thrill within her; she was swept into a kind of flight, her mind whisked somewhere else for a spell. All about and some place until she heard a burst of raucous laughter. An old woman's laugh, coming from the old farm, Hóll. Was she being laughed at? Standing still like a fool, deep in her silly thoughts, not moving, there in the middle of the street. She looked up and saw no one but was still embarrassed as she hurried on home.

She ran upstairs, threw herself on the bed and continued to imagine her future, staying there until her father came home. Then she rushed back down and was still fervid enough to deliver the speech she hadn't dared make for quite some time. A speech packed with questions and explanations. When would it be her turn to travel abroad? She talked, too, about her mother's promises about education and all the things she knew she shouldn't bring up. And so she stood courageously before her father, her hands set on her hips as a sign of willpower. But his eyes looked past her as usual. Money. He didn't have enough right now, not even enough to send her brother abroad this fall. Her immediate response: She had a little money she'd received for sewing and other things. Kristín and Páll had often invited her to come to Edinburgh and spend a winter with them.

"Oh, as if they don't have enough already," Brandur responded, mentioning some troubles the couple were going through, and that the last he'd heard they'd been in a bloody mess. Then he went into his office, but before he closed the door behind him he said something about castles in the sky. Said they were little people in a small town. He asked why she wanted to go somewhere where she would be even littler and more insignificant than she really was. Where she'd be less than nothing.

She went upstairs, undressed, and lay down. Less than nothing? She pulled the blanket over her head, closed her eyes, and tried to imagine what such a person would look like. Of course, she didn't see a thing, not until she was about to drift off. An image appeared above her, something colossal, like earth torn up to show roots that swung long and slender in a count of thousands back and forth as its surface passed over her. And when this gigantic piece of earth was far enough away she saw that a large, gleaming castle stood on it. It was blue and white. It was a castle in the sky.

The Arena

She knocked on the door for a third time and finally someone came and opened it a crack. Mrs. Popp hid her face half behind the door, wearing a strange expression, as if she didn't care for visitors. Sigurlína explained she'd come to meet Silvía and just then the door was torn open and her friend welcomed her. She led her into the living room and said she had something for her. Watson and his people had returned to Reykjavík, and she had been asked to find two girls to help with a party on board the *Arena* before the group sailed back to England the next morning. When Sigurlína, for some reason, pretended to be indifferent, Silvía said that she herself was going to go aboard and do some tasks, just a little, even though she didn't think it was her job to serve others. Sigurlína felt as though she'd been told that the job was good enough for her, but she was too excited, she couldn't help smiling as Silvía took both of her hands and told her to meet her at five o'clock. They would be ferried out ahead of the Icelandic guests.

She went out to Lækjartorg Square, looked around and admired the ships in the harbor. She had never been on board a foreign ship. She thought of Watson, tried to conjure his face, but it wouldn't come to her. Next, she turned into Pósthússtræti and walked toward Parliament; Brandur had asked her to come by and write out a few cards for a new exhibition case. As she walked, she wondered if she'd had Watson's face in mind too long, if that explained why she had a hard time picturing it. But then it was suddenly there, not inside her head but right in front of her. The eyes, the beard, the hair, everything emerging from the Parliament building. She was so startled she almost bowed low before greeting him in English. But that greeting wasn't received by anyone but the door in front of her, for Watson had already rushed away. She turned and saw him walking briskly along Pósthússtræti, taking swift steps. Hadn't he seen her? Where was he coming from? Had he been with her father?

She realized she probably wouldn't have much time to help her father if she was going to be at Popp the merchant's pier at the appointed time. And if she went straight home, she would also avoid having to ask his permission. She always found it suited her better to write messages on slips of paper: it was in his nature to try to stop her plans, but he didn't interfere if he wasn't given the chance. So she turned around and headed home, trying to get into a rhythm despite the sole of one of her shoes sagging off. It was pretty clear that she wouldn't be wearing these boots tonight; her sheepskin slippers would have to do. She didn't know what Silvía herself was planning, but Sigurlína intended to wear her old costume: jacket with the white chemise. Her new apron, the tassel cap, and a black scarf.

And dressed thus, Sigurlína balanced in Pétur's boat as the waves came. In front of her, the rope ladder swung back and forth until she reached out for it. She climbed the first rung but slipped on the wet surface and would have fallen back down into the boat if she hadn't held tight to the ropes. Now she more resolutely ascended the ship's side, the waves below her, and she didn't pause until she reached the deck. And just as she was about to clamber over the rail, she was pulled up and hauled down to the deck by two sailors, with accompanying moans and men's laughter. Next came Silvía and then the third girl, Steingerður Jónsdóttir, Stappa for short.

The *Arena* was decorated with lanterns and pennants. From the deck, the girls were led into a small dining room where a table had been set and from there down to the kitchen. No one was in there; the surfaces were in complete chaos. There were two large pots on the stove. Sailors began to bring in boxes. One of them seemed to be the cook, and he ordered them, using brusque hand gestures more than words, to get to their feet and grab bowls. They were to ferry them to the dining room. There were no serving aprons to put on; Silvía was in any case quite against dressing in maid's clothing. But Sigurlína still thought she was better off in her costume with its cloth apron than Silvía and Stappa were in their satin dresses.

A babble of voices and noise carried down from the dining room, and when Sigurlína and Stappa each brought up their soup tureen, the guests were sitting at the table. A young boy, probably part of the crew, poured drinks into the glasses. Sigurlína held on to the large bowl and waited to be able to place it down. She regarded the banquet table. It was a strange sight. Watson was sitting there with Kristína Jóns by his side. What was she doing there? Wearing all these necklaces and this smile that Sigurlína had never seen her wear before? Next to them sat the Wilsons, and then came Miss Baker and Mr. Johnson. Next to Johnson sat the Poet, who nodded eagerly over something that his seatmate whispered to him. Opposite them sat Icelandic officials and some of their wives. Two of them dressed in Icelandic national costume, skautbúningur. All at once it struck Sigurlína as bizarre, as if these outfits didn't belong here, on board this ship. But it was the Governor's costume that stood out the most inside this small, low-ceilinged room. Those enormous epaulettes. That headgear. Those snow-white feathers rising from the headdress. And Sigurlína felt like he was aware that, even though he took up all this space, all that decoration somehow made him small compared to the rather modest clothing worn by the Americans.

She next ascended the steep stairs with a large dish full of fish. When she entered the hall, the Poet had risen to his feet to offer a toast to Mr. Wilson. She heard him talking about foreign educational trends coming to Iceland, progress and the like.

When the tables were set, Silvía sent a message to the cook that they wouldn't clean anything while on board. That hadn't been part of the agreement. And now Silvía and Stappa were heading up on deck where the guests were gathering to join in a song; judging from the noises carrying down, you could work out that some of the party had had a little too much wine. The chef and the waiter had both disappeared from the kitchen and Sigurlína stood there alone. She organized the dishes, felt like they hadn't done anything. She wiped her hands and face and went out of the kitchen and upstairs.

When she entered the corridor that led to the dining room, she sensed someone walking behind her. She looked into the dark but saw no one. She kept going, but as she was about to push open the door at the end of the corridor, someone grabbed her shoulder. Lightly. She turned around. In front of her stood a man. He seized her in both hands and pulled her forward, in through a narrow door, toward a small dim light. The man was Watson and this was his cabin. His face was strange in the light, formidable and rough so close up, and his hair seemed black to her, and his eyes too. He reeked of schnapps. She thought about breaking free but felt peculiar, felt she couldn't move, held by some pleasurable feeling which was quite different from the one she had felt with Jón when they had been alone in the alley. Some witlessness was playing about inside her head, two things she didn't recognize were happening at once, some swell of both pleasure and disgust that was magnified when Watson lifted her apron, her skirt and undergarments, bent down and stroked his coarse beard up along her neck and whispered something in her ear that she didn't understand. But it sounded ugly. He had his hands around her hips and gently pushed her back and down into his bunk. She put her hands under herself and was about to get up but got nowhere, because Watson himself had now crawled into the bunk and was on his knees on top of her. Involuntarily, her left foot sought out the man's shoulder but when she tried to push him away, he firmly grabbed her tiny sheepskin shoe, rubbed its pointed toe against his nose and smiled. "Don't be a prissy old maid." Then he let go, pushed her skirt farther up her stomach and sat carefully down on her middle, began to rock back and forth as if in a trance, his eyes closed.

She whispered, "Mr. Watson?" And then it was as if he had been knocked down, aimed right at her body so that she threw herself onto her side and covered her face. But his crotch was still locked to her waist, held even more fast, a great weight, as his breathing deepened. Sigurlína lay gravely still. She was starting to quake. She no longer felt the strange bliss that had fastened itself around her body a moment ago, only self-revulsion as she lay there under this foreign body. She thought she had to get out of there as soon as possible, but she felt she had no power to crawl away from this terrible load.

A symposium in Reykjavík, March 1897. At the beginning of the evening.

"Nonsense! It's utterly childish to think you can base secure, stable relationships between nations on such a device! And why do we need such fast-moving communication with the outside world anyway?"

He had been the last to arrive at the meeting, turning up midway through this outburst from the Historian, having almost been hit by a sled full of rocks which some wretch in sheepskin shoes had lost control of on the slopes of Bakarabrekka as he headed down to Austurstræti, where the new bank building was being built. But the Governor had welcomed the young Editor nonetheless, and conversation soon turned from radios and wireless telegraph to the country's flag and coat of arms until the head of the house formally greeted his guests and called their meeting to order. He hadn't directly spelled out his agenda, but began his narration by recalling a small incident:

"This past autumn, an event took place: the scholar Brandur Jónsson's daughter sailed away from Iceland." Then he stoops down, lowering his voice: "Some even go so far as to say that she fled the country under cover of night. She is currently believed to be in Scotland."

"Sigurlína?" asks the Poet, with a troubled sorrow, as if he himself somehow suffered from the young girl's actions.

Governor: "Yes, that's her name. An intelligent girl but quite singular in many respects."

Historian: "I do not know this woman."

Chief Justice: "Petite, fair-haired. Not unpretty but a little unruly."

Treasurer: "Yes, fickle. Somewhat insolent, too."

Priest: "It's all that hard work at home."

Chief Justice: "Her father's slave."

Poet: "Yes, but still out and about with foreign men. Trying out her English. It's like that with the women in this town. In that regard, she's unpatriotic. She's also been working hard to sell them all kinds of frippery, sewing and knitting."

Priest: "But isn't that patriotic—and practical?"

Poet: "Socks and other nonsense?"

Chief Justice: "Isn't she sedulously working to make some good of herself?"

Poet: "Yes, of course. But it's all worthless because everything she does is governed by daydreams and her scattered mind; there's no way all that industry is headed anywhere. What's more, she fled. Causing her father great distress."

The Historian doesn't speak again, just shrugs his shoulders as though he'd rather discuss something more important, and looks to the Editor, who is also silent, but for a completely different reason. But just as the Historian is about to change the subject, the maid walks into the room with a

43

silver tray in her hands. The men are all in good cheer, their attention entirely on the brimful liquor glasses. This little ceremony will take some time.

A Great Deed

"Mr. Watson?" Someone was outside the door. Her legs jerked and she began to kick herself free, cycling them up in the air. She pressed both hands against one of the man's shoulders and slid her small frame out from under the smelly lump.

She was quick to throw herself up onto the berth so she could fix her jacket and cap, but then felt something stuck to her buttocks. Something rock hard. She felt around and discovered it under her skirt. She got up and shook her skirt until the thing fell to the floor. It glinted in the dim light. To her, it looked like something from Watson's outfit, a belt buckle, something like that. She reached for it and held it under the lantern that hung on the wall. Then, she heard her name called, and at the same time she realized what the little thing was. She stroked her face with one hand, squeezed the object in the other, and hurried out.

Up on the deck she saw someone helping Silvía over the ship's railing. Sigurlína noticed she wore a strange expression but when Silvía disappeared overboard, she concealed the object under her jacket and walked toward the captain, who helped her off. Her legs trembled at every step, and once down in the boat she had to go on her haunches and almost crawl to the thwart, where she sat opposite Pétur, her feet a little to the side, on top of a tangled mess of net so she could keep them out of the puddle that had collected below the plank. Silvía and Stappa sat behind her. Both stone silent. From the deck, occasional shouts and cries could be heard. The guests seemed to have scattered around the ship; some were perhaps already back ashore.

Pétur rowed away from the ship. That's when Sigurlína started to shake, so intensely that he looked away and stared at the moon. She stared at the moon too and tried to think into the future. The *Arena* would be out of port before Watson came to his senses. She would never see him again. She ought to obliterate the memory of his conduct and her stupid reaction, not torment herself over it. If she had let him dishonor her, that was fate; someone had to fall into the trap that was his cabin. She looked at little Pétur, and at her little town as it lay behind him in the autumn darkness. By the time they'd eased up to the pier, she had stopped trembling.

She said goodbye to the girls and walked home. Along the way, she prepared the speech to her father. He wouldn't mention the fact that she had gone out to the ship with the girls without letting him know, but he would deem her actions regarding the object just and appropriate. That's what she was thinking as she entered the kitchen and decided to disclose her discovery of the theft to him. She slipped her hand inside her jacket and was about to utter the words when she realized what his first question would be: How had she come by this thing? Had the thief Watson dropped it on the floor or the deck and she simply cleaned it up? Had she gone into his pocket and fished it up from there? Or did she find it in his cabin? What the hell was she doing in there?

Sigurlína squeezed the object in her palm, took a few steps back and hurried upstairs. She had better let it be. What had she been thinking? She buried the object deep at the bottom of her chest. She probably had no choice but to try to take it back to the museum before Brandur noticed it had disappeared. But that would probably never work; her father was going to finish the display case containing the new discoveries as soon as tomorrow. And without doubt the ancient brooch, which her father had called a cape clasp, would be among the chief treasure.

This shall be mine!

It had been two days since Sigurlína brought the brooch home from Mr. Watson's cabin. During that time, Brandur hadn't been to the museum but stayed at home to complete a project. In order to succeed in her mission—to return her find—she'd need her father not only to make a trip to the museum but also to ask her to accompany him. And finally, on the third day, when that seemed to be turning out as she'd hoped, old Þórður happened to knock on their door to bring them some dead birds, unwittingly derailing Sigurlína's plan; when the old man had taken his leave, and Brandur was about to set off, she asked if she should come down and help with the display, he pointed at the birds and said she probably had enough to be getting on with at home today. She said the birds could wait; she would pluck them tonight. But before her father could react there was a second knock at the door. This time it was Þórdís. She had come to pick up her ribbons. Sigurlína hurried upstairs to fetch them before her father left the house but soon realized the ribbons were not there. She had sold them to Watson and company!

She was wondering how to get out of this when she heard the door slam shut again. Brandur was gone. She had missed the opportunity to slip the brooch back and now she was left with nothing but trying to explain to Þórdís what had happened to her ribbons.

And the birds, of course. Should she start in on them? Or begin making new ribbons for Þórdís, who had been given the explanation that Sigurlína couldn't find them anywhere—they had simply evaporated. Sigurlína decided to begin inside the kitchen and to try to calm her thoughts. Pluck, singe, scrape, wash, and dry. Cut off the head, wings, and legs. Remove the guts. Then, she hung the birds up in the pantry and started thinking about dinner. But she couldn't think it through because she knew her father had realized by now the ancient brooch had disappeared from the museum. There was no other way out except to tell him the truth.

But Brandur came home that night without mentioning anything. And he went back down again and returned home again without bringing up the missing object. Wasn't he concerned? He didn't seem any more anxious than usual. It was as if nothing had happened, leading Sigurlína to begin to wonder if all this was her imagination, some misunderstanding—but when she reached down into her trunk to check on her haul, she had no doubt that the brooch that stuck to her rear in the American businessman's cabin was the one she had handled in the museum. Was it possible that her father thought the brooch was lost and that he wanted to wait to announce that until it was found? Sigurlína thought that this might well be the case; her father was working on a complete list of all the collection's artifacts and there were definitely many thousands of them. Hither and thither in boxes and chests. Perhaps in his mind he believed the brooch misplaced; in the meantime, she still had a chance to return it. But to do so would involve waiting a while, because now Brandur was on his way north to investigate the ruins of some houses and to inquire into antiquities on farms. In fact, Sigurlína herself scarcely had time to think about the brooch right this moment: she was preparing for a dance that was to be held tomorrow night in a new assembly hall by the pond, Tjörnin. A masked ball.

She had half expected Jón to take her to the ball; he had asked whether she was going. But when she heard that he had ridden out to Bessastaðir with his father, she asked her brother to accompany her. He had been rather silent since his return from the north but agreed to her request, with the caveat that he wasn't going to dress up in some costume for this rubbish. Apart from her black eye mask, Sigurlína hadn't intended to wear a funny costume, just her gown and her golden hairband.

It was rather cloudy when the siblings headed into town. A few people had gathered in front of the hall to inspect the guests' fashions. The sight was richly decorative. Several of the boys had wrapped white linen around themselves; one of them wore a red turban around his head. There were clowns, flower fairies, a naval officer, a soldier, and all sorts of costumes which were more than colorful but difficult to tell what they were meant to be. Girls had sewn flowers on their dresses and hats. Inga Hansen was more original, wearing a top hat. Sigurlína gave her brother an elbow to show she'd noticed he was enjoying seeing some of his friends among the guests. Her friends were there, too: Silvía had a folding fan over her face while Stappa was a witch wearing a homemade conical hat. Sigurlína alone wore the Icelandic national costume, the kyrtill.

She danced with her brother and some of his friends. It was all very informal, and she felt a sense of chaos in the organization of the gathering. For a while, the musical accompaniment seemed to be getting out of rhythm; she couldn't work out what was being played on the piano. But she had a good time—up until it was almost the end of the evening. She was standing with some other girls in a corner of the hall where drinks were being served. She quenched her thirst and looked across the room. A vivid image of young people wearing badly-made costumes, many of which had begun to look the worse for wear after the evening's frolicking. Right then, a man entered the scene. Jón Jónsson. Wearing dark clothes with a collar and cuffs. So beautifully neat, slender, well combed. Had he not ridden to Bessastaðir after all, like his mother had indicated?

Sigurlína set down her glass and was about to walk toward him but stopped when she saw who was at his side. A woman in a black silk dress with bright red ribbons. It was the Danish woman. Sigurlína hadn't realized she was so tall. And so pretty, despite being older than her companion. The two of them gave her a friendly look, but instead of returning the greeting she rushed out of the hall and was outside before she knew it. If she had been trying to dispel the reality that now dawned on her—that Jón was clearly engaged to this strange woman Sigurlína hadn't heard anyone in town mention or gossip about—it was too late. She hardly knew which was worse: the disappointment that this man had slipped through her hands or the shame that followed from reacting so stupidly to seeing them. Could she go back in and pretend nothing had happened, correct this ill-conceived behavior? Probably not. There would be sneering, suppressed laughter.

She could imagine what the reaction had been when she ran out of the room. Damn it all. Where was her brother? And at that moment she heard his name being mentioned. Some of his friends were standing up against the wall, smoking and talking. About him. About his travels: "He's sailing this fall, yes."

Sigurlína looked straight ahead: Was her brother headed to Copenhagen after all? Why hadn't he told her? Had her father made clear he would be the one to reveal the news when he returned to Reykjavík? But where had the money suddenly come from? She looked around. The boys had gone back inside. She stood there alone in the twilight. On the wet ground, wearing the gown her mother had sewn for her before her Confirmation and which still fit her. The air was cold and moist after the evening's downpour. Her shawl was inside the hall, and there it would have to stay. She wasn't going back inside. But she couldn't stand here any longer, either.

She lifted her white skirt, tore off her mask, and ran out onto Kirkjustræti and from there into Aðalstræti. The street had become one floating sea of mud. She tried to tip-toe from cobble to cobble and to hurry as fast as she could because it was starting to rain again. But she had reached the end of the street and was about to jump over one of the watery troughs when, worst of luck, she slipped on the mud and fell backward. Right on her ass because she couldn't manage to stop herself with her hands, so tightly was she holding onto her skirt with one hand, her mask in the other. She had not wanted the white silk to touch the earth, but now she had thoroughly soiled her costume. When she got back to her feet she heard a low laugh just behind her. She looked around and saw where the brawler Kristján was going through the gate at the Duus house. He splashed on along the street in his sloppy coat, the housekeeper following him.

Sigurlína tramped onward without caring any longer about the earth below her. In the darkness she tormented herself and thought of Jón, how elegant he had been there amid the slobs, the sweaty and ruddy townsfolk. She thought of her brother, of her father. Then she thought of Watson, and by that time she'd reached home. She undressed, tried to clean most of the dirt from her dress, and pretended to be asleep when her brother opened the door to her room. But she wasn't headed toward some dream that would allow her to flee the hopelessness of her existence for the night. She was on her way somewhere completely different, even though she had no idea where. And she wasn't going to ask her mother for advice by staring into her face behind the glass in the frame above the bed.

She got up from her bed, sat down at her table and grabbed a different glass: the old hand mirror that her grandfather had given her grandmother, who had refused to look into it. Sigurlína had inherited the mirror because, unlike her grandmother, she enjoyed seeing her own face in the flecked old glass. But now her face was swollen with weeping. Would she dissolve away before she could finally escape her misery? She felt she couldn't possibly be any more alone in the world than here in this little town, this little house, within this little room. She looked at the wall and thought of the face that sometimes appeared on it in the dark, gaping to swallow her deep inside. By now she thought she had figured out whose face it was, what it was after. Wouldn't it be better to be less than nothing somewhere at the heart of the world than to be nothing at its periphery, not even aware of how diminutive she was? Not until some foreigner lies down on top of you and starts tittering? She looked at herself through Watson's staring eyes, lying there with one foot up in the air, powerless in her sheepskin shoes, hapless with the check apron up around her waist, defenseless with the tassel falling on her cheek, the tassel held in a cylinder foreigners mistook for a telescope. And how long was she going to remain stuck in place? No doubt until her father took his leave of this earthly plane. Had he ever given her any other purpose than waiting on him, providing assistance to him until the bitter end? And when would that be? Twenty years' time? Maybe thirty? The thought jostled about inside her head. She got up, ran downstairs, went into her father's office. Where the hell was it? She placed her hands on one of the piles on the desk and began sweeping the papers in all directions, searching for the letter. For a moment she almost thought she had dreamed it all, but then, practically at that very moment, she saw the letter floating slowly down to the floor; she plucked it from the air, the thin piece of stationery, and whispered as loudly as she dared, in a voice she hardly knew as her own: "This shall be mine!"

II

Burgdorf. Riverside Drive.

A bestiary. A book of beasts in a vellum-skin manuscript; English, from the mid twelfth century. He takes the treasure from its wrapping carefully, with an expert's fastidiousness. A sense of anticipation thrums within him, a tension of which he never tires, the force behind his silent, lonely existence. He is the German-born Franz W. Hoffmann, owner of the largest rare book and manuscript collection in the Northeast, one of the richest figures in all of Manhattan's wealthiest communities. A scholar of medieval Europe, his recent passion has tended more toward acquiring old books and manuscripts than to studying the history they contain.

Hoffmann sets the manuscript on a large table in the center of the room. No, not exactly: this room is more of a hall, maybe even a hundred square meters, two levels, with a platform that runs around all four walls and in places recedes into dark corners where books hide, countless books carefully catalogued in impressive leather volumes, which lie on the table along with his latest catch, the bestiary.

It's past midnight but almost impossible to tell the difference between night and day in this windowless expanse; its vaulted bas-relief ceiling has finely wrought imagery with embellishments around a fresco that draws inspiration from Germanic mythology. Here is where Hoffmann holes up eighteen hours a day, indulging his noble obsession, feeding his gentle madness while fondly caressing his collection. He's of average height, with coarse features, slender, skinny even. His thin gray hair is combed back to his neck, his beard the same color, rough and thick and hiding all the expressions his face might make beneath its bony, curved nose. The bright eyes are set deep, as though they have seen everything they wish to see. Hoffmann is seventy.

In the entryway to the library stand the Greek gods made of marble; a limestone staircase leads from there to the building's second floor, which hosts numerous living quarters, in one of which lives Hermine, Hoffmann's bedridden mother. She is one hundred and has been lying in her canopy bed for more than a year, being shifted regularly as needed. Her room has two floor-to-ceiling windows on either side of a large fireplace with ornate stonework. Everything here is in the style of Louis XVI, except perhaps Caspar the Magi, of average height and carved from poplar with gilding on his jacket. He is Moorish, from a medieval monastery in Baden-Baden, and has followed Hermine's family about for a long time. These days he stands in the corner beside her bed, watching over her when she's not being visited by the two house servants or the doctor who calls to see the old lady once a week. Hoffmann habitually visits his mother before going to bed, but tonight he forgot about her amid his interest in the new manuscript. So

Hermine fell asleep on her own after one of the maids had seen to her as usual.

Those are the happenings in the fifty-room house by the Hudson River, far from the city mansions of the wealthy Manhattanites. Hoffmann had this house built shortly after his father died, naming it after his father's hometown, its location a kind of declaration of his disdain toward the affluent community to which he certainly belonged, those uber-wealthy people who had built palaces on the wide streets running down Central Park's east side, their vanity and arrogance unbridled. He no longer had anything to do with his fellow citizens; most of the people Hermine had met upon arriving to New York from Germany with her husband, the steel producer Hoffmann the Elder, were now dead. But their descendants had become many times richer than their ancestors and lived surrounded by wealth. Especially the new members who had joined the group with the rising generation.

The accumulation of wealth in this great financial center of New York City both feeds and is founded on a new kind of lifestyle, which ever-increasing factory production makes possible, all of it driven by an enormous population increase: migration. Since the time the Hoffmanns settled on Manhattan, the area's population has nearly tripled. On a normal day more than seven thousand newcomers land on Ellis Island to enter the newly-built immigration station. Ships clog the harbor; others make for port. One of them is caught in a storm off the coast of Nova Scotia and is climbing out of a ten-meter-deep wave trough, only to fall down again. The *Buchanan*, a nine-thousand-ton steamship from Glasgow. The ship's been sailing for more than a week, with about a thousand passengers on board, people from sundry nations who are tossing about in their living quarters, inside the first-class lounge, inside the narrow sleeping berths of the lower decks. And in second class, in a four-person cabin, a young woman lies, seriously ill. She lies there in the upper bunk and holds onto the rail with a death grip.

This is Sigurlína, and she is a long way from home. She's been traveling for about four weeks, since leaving Reykjavík the morning after the costume ball. That fateful event. And it all happened at an alarming speed, precipitated by the letter she retrieved from her father's desk: She dashed up to her room, rooted about in the clutter, peered out of her bedroom window into the darkness at the water's edge, shouted to herself, "James!" then said the name again, quieter, as she pulled out her trunk and put almost everything she owned inside: clothes, a few books, two English novels, photographs, a little bit of needlework, her small wooden chest containing her money and some letters—and, at the bottom, the old brooch, the damnable brooch she is stuck with and desperately needs to get rid of, preferably to make disappear, to bury on the beach, to throw into the sea, yes, throw it into the sea, what an idea, so she started to get ready, to put on her travel clothes, the striped dress she'd bought last year and the black jacket she had sewn and not yet used and which she buttoned up as she knelt down at one end of the room, bent over by her uncontrollable thoughts and irrational decisions, movements those decisions necessitated, decisions which hardened her mind as she turned back to get the picture of her mother that was hanging on the wall, putting it in her lap as the living room clock struck four A.M., and she lay back down but did not let go of the picture, setting it on her breast with her hands clasped on top of it until she suddenly woke to a commotion downstairs, her brother getting up and going out of the house with a slam of the door, so she jumped to her feet and started to get on with things for the second time, confused but resolute, placing the picture of her mother inside the trunk and closing it before pushing it out of the room and onto the landing at the top of the stairs, a small landing, she pushed it too far out and caused the trunk to topple and launch down the steep stairs and hit the wooden floor with such a bang that she cried out and ran into her father's study so she could look out the window and see if the noise had woken any of the townspeople, but when she saw no movement in the next house she sat down at the desk and wrote her father a short letter, setting it on top of a wooden box that stood at one corner of the desk, then went into the pantry to prepare provisions—two slices of salted meat, some liver sausage, a whole Christmas cake, a morsel of cheese and all the remaining bread—and then the clock struck eight and she knew that now the time had come, so she went out and called two boys loafing about in the street and asked them to help her get her luggage down to the pier where a boat was docked and the rower—he didn't ask any questions—was ready to ferry her out to the harbor where the *James*, a livestock ship, lay at anchor, with the ship's captain on the upper deck shaking his head and claiming to have no room for a woman and Sigurlína down in the boat insisting on being allowed to climb aboard to explain her mission to Scotland and the impromptu preparation for her voyage, and she kept on with such zeal and despair that the captain couldn't help but let her aboard, couldn't help but listen to this delicate little woman tell one complex, incomprehensible story, standing there with banknotes in one hand, which sealed it for the captain, who agreed to let her embark and who guided her to a shoebox cabin next to his own, saying that she would have to make do, either this windowless closet or the hold full of sheep and horses, but while Sigurlína was clambering in and her trunk was being hoisted aboard, the story of the sudden departure of Brandur Jónsson's daughter was just setting sail on its own journey around town, departing the shoreline and traveling along the town's streets where people looked ponderingly into the air or gave a sharp intake of breath, certain something was afoot, judging her not at all safe on board this ship which was about to weigh anchor and set its prow to the south, spurred by a gathering north wind to commence its seven-day voyage to Scotland with Sigurlína cramped in a tiny teapot of a room reading Scott and Dickens then Scott again, falling asleep to the sheep's bleats, the horses' neighs, waking up in the night, feeling peculiar and poorly and wondering, "What have I done?," then eating her cheese, her liver sausage, her bread, her Christmas cake and her salted meat and drinking the coffee the cabin boy brought her once a day and that was almost her sole contact with the crew because she hardly set foot outside her door except the few occasions she staggered outside but the air inside the cabin was so stale—the space was more like a storage closet than a real cabin—that being outside up on deck almost confused her as she breathed the sea air and had a hard time accepting the captain's greeting as he looked at her like he thought maybe she had lost her mind though he still bid her farewell when they made port in Leith and she held her head high as she climbed up into the carriage to head to Edinburgh and she thought she was all set when outside the station she handed the driver a two-year-old envelope with Páll and Kristín's address on it and thus set off along the narrow streets of the city toward the house, which of course looked very different from what she had imagined, and what's more it was actually no longer their home according to the young lady who came to the door and directed her further down the street where another woman sent her further up the street and so on and so forth until the carriage reached a completely different place, a crumbling house where no one came to the door until Sigurlína had walked around back, down some stairs, and knocked on a black door that opened slowly after she had rained blows on it with all the emotion of someone wandering around alone in the dark in a strange country—and upon seeing her Icelandic friend, she broke down, and didn't notice his appearance, how wretched he looked, didn't notice it until she had come in and heard the man's sad story, how his wife, Kristín, had run off with an Englishman and was as far as he knew lodging in London, how he had mostly been all alone here, and she could read in his eyes how happy he was to see his fellow Icelander after many months isolation, it was as if coming to the end of his tale and realizing he was no longer alone refreshed him, he jumped to his feet and made coffee and was rather impressed by his young friend's plan, and, yes, of course, he was going to help her with everything she needed to get on board the *Buchanan* departing from Glasgow to New York in about a week.

And that journey had unfolded according to plan up to the present moment: There are four occupied bunks in the cabin and Sigurlína is at the end of her rope. She needs to get out. The corridor in front of the cabin is full of passengers so she heads up the other way, but finds herself in a corridor she has not walked down before. She fumbles about in the dark until she comes to the stairs, but going up she loses her bearings. She walks along the passages this way and that for a long time; she goes up one flight of stairs and then another until she finds her way out to the upper deck. At first the door won't budge, but then it's suddenly torn open, and Sigurlína falls forward and the sea barrages her with great force. She lies there, half inside the doorway, and is just getting to her feet when another wave crashes against the ship and knocks her back down again, submerging her. She scrambles across the deck with her body hunkered low in the trough of the wave and manages to grab the railing before she's swept over it, and down to the deck below. With effort, she finds the floor again, and when the ship rights itself, she lies on her stomach with her skirt in disarray, and looks over the ship, at the passengers huddling together in a single knot, holding on to posts and poles, whatever keeps them from getting washed into the ocean. When the ship straightens out once more, she lets go for a moment, slips a hand into the outer pocket of her soaking wet skirt. She feels for the thing she must not lose. One small, snow-white hand clasped around the handrail pole, tightening her grip when the ship explodes with the waves once again, and then she finally finds what she is looking for: a letter addressed to Brandur Jónsson, director of The Antiquarian Collection, and dated early autumn this year. A letter in an envelope which has the sender's name and address written on the flap: Dr. Franz W. Hoffmann. Burgdorf. Riverside Drive. New York City.

*A symposium in Reykjavík, March 1897. In the
middle of the evening.*

"A peculiar man," says the Priest, once the Governor returns
to the living room—from the toilet—to resume his mission
of reminding his guests about a man named Franz W. Hoffmann, a man who appears, along with Sigurlína, to play no
little role in the issue that has been put on the night's agenda.

"Roughly so," says the Treasurer, and leans back as soon
as he has extended his hand to the Poet, as if giving him the
floor, soliciting words in support of his own remarks. And
the Poet responds immediately by stroking his long beard:
"That was an ugly matter."

"*Codex Scardensis?*" It is the Historian asking, getting
only a "What?" from his comrades each in competition with
the other until the young Editor finally raises his voice: "The
Sagas of the Apostles from Skarð disappeared several decades
ago and have now turned up in England."

"But he must have taken something away in his trunk,
that gent?" asks the Historian, and the Poet answers tasteful-
ly: "Yes, he was rather capacious in his purchases of manu-

scripts and old prints." And to these words the men respond with movements of their heads and half-sounds, but again the Editor stops this creaking transfer of vague thoughts, and then becomes a little nervous and has to suck down some air: "How does this American bibliophile connect to Sigurlína's departure?"

But before the Governor can answer that question, he needs, he says, to introduce a third person, a woman: "Brenda Anderson? Does anyone here know that name in connection with research into the life of Guðríður Þorbjarnardóttir?" No, the Governor had not expected so.

Sigurlína from Iceland

Even though her dress, the best one, had hung in the cabin all night, the skirt was still damp after yesterday's hardships. Why had she put it on before the ship docked? Thank god she had her new hat on her head, the one she bought in Edinburgh; that little straw boater with pink flowers on the brim gave her a bit of confidence as she stood amid the throng inside the large, cold immigration building on Ellis Island. Physically examined, with a tag on the front of her breast, she answered countless questions, strange questions, explaining why she was there—but once she showed them her letter, she was allowed through.

A boat sailed up to 42nd Street and there she hired a carriage. Now comes a moment of truth, she thought, though she was too tired to take in her immense surroundings or fear her destination. But when she got there, she was hit full force by what was happening to her. Burgdorf. Maybe she should have known that a house with such a name must be enormous. But still, something was not right, this couldn't be the place, so she gave the envelope with the address back to the driver, and he, a short, fat older man with a top hat on his head, nodded that it was, and took the trunk down from the carriage and carried it along a paved path that led to the house. Sigurlína followed, looking around. Once the man had left her luggage in front of a huge, windowless door, and Sigurlína had paid, he was off.

Now it was just her and the trunk. First, she adjusted her hat and smoothed her skirt. Adjusted the hat back, stroked the skirt a little smoother, clenched both fists, stretched out her right hand and prepared to do what seemed impossible; the carved woodwork swallowed her hesitant blows as they ratted lightly against the door. How could such a door open? There was no doorknob. She noticed a small button set within a golden rosette on the stone frame to the right: a bell. She pressed the button, but too gently, not knowing what would happen if she pressed her finger all the way down. But she suddenly backed out of that act as someone started to open the door, revealing the joints in this massive slab of wood.

A man wearing black clothes and a white collar stood in the doorway, bidding her good morning, bowing hesitantly and not very deeply. She swallowed and returned his greeting. She said her name was Sigurlína. She had come from Iceland to meet with Mr. Hoffmann.

"From Iceland?" The servant smiled benevolently but then cleared his throat thoroughly once he set eyes on the trunk behind her. He shifted about in the doorway for a while, until another man appeared out of the darkness behind him. It was the master of the house, there was no doubt about it, given the way the servant retreated a few steps, stepping aside as if to prepare for the next part of this unexpected visit. Hoffmann walked forward; Sigurlína looked down at the doorstep, offered a greeting, and extended her hand. The letter. Hoffmann accepted the envelope and invited Sigurlína to enter. To close the door with the trunk still outside seemed somewhat not right, so the servant, the steward, drew it into the lobby under his master's restless gaze. Hoffmann opened the envelope enclosing the letter. The letter he wrote himself about three months ago:

Burgdorf.
Riverside Drive
June 27th 1896

Dear Mr. Jónsson,

Allow me to begin by refreshing your memory of our first acquaintance. Some ten years ago I traveled to Iceland in the company of a German colleague of mine to visit the major historical sites of your country. At the end of our trip we stayed in Reykjavik where I made several visits to the library and the Antiquarian Collection, then housed at the Parliament House, and where we discussed among other things the future of the museum and the library. I am ever so grateful to you for these inspiring conversations and exchanges. Since my visit to Iceland I have become ever more interested in the history and literature of your country, and for several years now I have directed my research entirely toward the documents relating to the Icelandic discovery of America, a subject that has recently attracted no small amount of attention in our society. Regrettably, this learned interest in Icelandic exploration has often taken the form of dubious theories and conjectures, as the original historical records have not been readily accessible. For that reason, partly, I have been working on an endeavor that aims to bring together information, contained in Icelandic literature, relative to the discovery of America by the Icelanders. And now to the purpose of my letter to you: I hereby kindly ask you to help me find an assistant, a native Icelander with sound knowledge of the Sagas, particularly those in question, skills in reading the texts from a photographic reproduction of the vellum manuscript (and paper manuscript in my possession), and substantial knowledge of the English language. The assistant will be provided with board and lodging here at my house along with payment for the period of one year at the least.

Respectfully yours,
your colleague,
Dr. Franz W. Hoffmann

Hoffmann looked up from his reading and looked inquiringly at Sigurlína, who spoke to the stone floor, loudly and clearly: "I'm your assistant."

It was Hoffmann's turn to look down at the floor. He ran his hand down his narrow face, tugged at his beard as if he wanted to rip it off, then looked up into the air, and asked, in a very low voice, where she had got this letter which was addressed to Mr. Jónsson. She said that the addressee,

Brandur, was her father; she read manuscripts and had all the knowledge and experience required in the letter. Was she sent by Brandur himself? No, Hoffmann decided not to ask and instead tried to explain to her that he could not put her to use. But he did not dare articulate the thought, felt it would be impolitic to say as much. And so time stood still a while, until the steward looked as though he was going to retreat, probably out of courtesy as much as any duties. Hoffmann immediately gave him a signal to stay and so to take part in the silence that now occupied the house's elegant hallway, a space too small for these unexpected events despite its enormous size. It was as if Hoffmann were thinking: What am I to do? At this very moment? He could not show an Icelander the door, not as a scholar in his field, and moreover this woman was the daughter of a man who had shown him exceptional hospitality and generosity when he visited their country. Could it be that Brandur was behind this? Did he feel he was owed a favor? All well and good. But where should he host this woman? Upstairs or down? What class is a female scribe from Iceland? Of a class with clerics or tutors? But no one like that had ever lived here, only masters and servants; he had not even thought his plans for the Icelandic assistant through to the end. Hoffmann did not know whether he was coming or going—nor did Sigurlína know whether she would be coming or going. Wasn't this something she should have foreseen? She had started smoothing her skirt again; it had dawned on her that her madness would leave her in disgrace. And had this heavy trunk not stood behind her in the hallway, she would have immediately excused her intrusion, said her goodbyes, and made her way out into whatever uncertain fate awaited her.

That could hardly be worse than having to breathe the atmosphere inside this glorious hall.

But then the tension finally eased. Hoffmann signaled to his steward, Mr. Gilbert, to carry her luggage up the stairs and for Sigurlína to follow. Up and into the blue room, as he called it. The order was both airy and hesitant, but it was obeyed firmly and without delay.

When the steward had closed the room's door behind her, Sigurlína sat down in a deep chair, cobalt blue. She was trembling, almost starting to sob. Out of shame but also relief. Something told her she was in safe hands; in fact, she must have suspected it all along. She would hardly have embarked on this long journey otherwise. But she hadn't imagined ending up at such a place as Hoffmann's residence. The poor don't travel to Iceland, but still, scholars aren't kings. Looking around was almost overwhelming and terribly uncomfortable for an uninvited guest. Would her actions be a dishonor to her father? The Icelandic nation? No, how could that be—her father had received a petition and she had done nothing but answer on his behalf. Wasn't she always finding solutions to all his tasks? Had Hoffmann specified that the assistant should be a man? It simply didn't look as bad as it had a few moments ago. But then the maid came in, set a tray on the table, and the way she said good morning, the way she smiled fleetingly at her, left Sigurlína with a nagging discomfort again. The girl's expression couldn't betoken anything but laughter once she left the room. Or, at least, was back inside the kitchen. Maybe a lot of people work here? Is the steward Gilbert down there telling the house's staff about the poor girl who knocked on the gentleman's door wearing a small flower hat on her head and with a large wooden trunk in tow? She took off her hat and found it tattered, not as fine as when she bought it in Edinburgh, with Páll waiting outside the store. Wouldn't it have been better to stay in Scotland and satisfy her burning need for the wider world there? A need she didn't fully comprehend, having finally arrived at her journey's end.

She had long since finished the tea and two cakes, had opened a narrow door to another room and found a large tub of shiny porcelain, two bowls, one presumably a toilet. She was looking out the window, out over the river, when there was a knock on the door. It was Gilbert; her dinner was waiting downstairs. He accompanied her there, then vanished. She sat alone, in a large kitchen that seemed equipped to cook food for little more than Hoffmann and his people. When she had finished the hash and vegetables, she found he was standing behind her: Gilbert, ready to take her back to her room.

She retrieved her nightgown from her trunk and crawled into bed. She was more dead than alive and could not puzzle out her fate. She ached at the softness beneath her. She closed her eyes. Then they merged into one, Hoffmann and philologist Konráð Gíslason.

Sigurlína had been directed to a seat. Hoffmann himself sat at a large desk about five meters from the chair in which she was sitting. He was flipping through some papers, pretending to flip through the papers, and then stated his case: He owed her father a debt of gratitude and would in the coming days ensure she found a position in the city as well as housing until she sailed home to Iceland in the spring. She may now return to her room. Or go out. She is, of course, free to travel.

Free to travel? But how could Sigurlína take any independent decisions inside this house? She hardly dared sit on her toilet, let alone get down into the bathtub. She didn't even know how to open the door out of the house; should she open it for herself, or even use the door through which she entered, or some other? And where was she supposed to go? Head up, north? Head down, south? She had to make do with sitting by her bedroom window and looking out at the river, at the women who rushed unhindered past on their bicycles. What could there be in this big city that would suit her? It could hardly be worse than the situation she found herself in inside this strange household.

In the morning she was called down again into Hoffmann's office. She thought he must have found something for her, but he didn't say anything about it, only directed her to a seat at a small desk next to his. Then he handed her a pile of letters. She was supposed to copy them out. He himself sat down to work; one meter between them. The tasks were easy to complete and moderately engaging. A letter about buying books, money, all sorts of other things that she didn't understand, but it was good to find purpose with the living and the silence that prevailed here, good to get his approval for her precision in writing, her clear and beautiful handwriting. He showed it with a gesture; this angular man didn't say more than was necessary. Had she now become his assistant? She didn't know.

But he half-hinted at it one day when he handed her a photograph of a vellum manuscript. It was *The Saga of Eirík the Red*. Roughly the same text she had previously copied from her father's paper manuscript. That made the reading and transcribing easier. She had finished five pages by six o'clock and felt she had proved what she had stated in the lobby a few days earlier. She was so happy when she stood up from her work that she almost wanted to say something more than her usual "thank you for today," but his silence was nerve-wracking, his presence so forceful, that Sigurlína, this brash and impulsive girl, had become introverted and sheepish. And the day they started translating and interpreting the text fragments from the manuscript, their communication amounted to just a few scattered words because by then Sigurlína herself had started to mimic him, to speak in cues and express her thoughts with small, neat gestures. Sometimes she found she could hardly feel for herself, that there was no reality beyond the text, nothing but this manuscript, these words, this story. But every once in a while Hoffmann would peek a sideways glance at her desk, watching her hand holding the pen as it ran along the paper, trying to make sense of words in a language she knew better than he did. That fact made her a bit unsteady, but also gave her strength.

Holda

She had finally found a way out. It lay along a long corridor off the kitchen and opened onto the back gardens. She first went down to the river, then through the gardens and further east, past cream-colored little palaces, and finally down to the south, where the settlement was denser and had a completely different appearance. Today she had walked all the way down to 20th Street and Broadway, where she bought herself a coat and a new hat, much bigger than the boater. She set it on her head on the way out of the store and became like all the other women floating along the streets on their way here and there, going nobody knows where. Everyone going somewhere. Everyone with their errand.

But where was Sigurlína heading? Just downtown some place then back up again. The excitement of wandering the streets gradually gave way to an emptiness, a sense of futility and disturbance. Perhaps, in spite of everything, it was better to belong to a small, unchanging community than to be invisible in the midst of all this life. Sometimes she made a game of bumping into people, just gently, but only to reap irritation and stares, the gaping faces of people from another world. She had traveled far but was still trapped in her own small world. She had fled, only to return.

She was dead on her feet when she returned north and walked toward Burgdorf. She went through the back gardens as usual. At the gate, she saw a large horse-drawn carriage and people walking out of the house. They held a coffin between them. The housekeepers stood by, Hoffmann in front. Sigurlína stopped at the gate. Suddenly she found her new coat too bulky, her hat too big. So she took it off but stood rooted to the spot as the men slid the coffin into the cart, which drove away from the house as soon as the people went back inside. Everyone except Mr. Gilbert, who stretched his hand toward Sigurlína and led her in while he briefly explained the strange sight.

It dawned on Sigurlína what her position in the house was. She knew she had a role here from day to day but she was not part of this household. People died here without her ever even knowing they'd existed. Maybe the house was full of people she didn't know? Dying people? She didn't even know if the death of the old lady, her master's elderly mother, called for a particular kind of grief; the silence inside this house couldn't be much heavier than it already was.

After she expressed her sympathy to her master and he politely accepted the insufficient platitude, life went on as if nothing had happened. Everything went off quite smoothly. She picked up some correspondence, transcribed it, and then laid it on his desk. Letters but also parcels. Old books and manuscripts. Out of a brown package this morning came a small envelope and a thick pile of densely written pages. Written on the front page, in decorative letters, was *Gudrid.*

The First Caucasian Mother in America. Sigurlína catalogued the manuscript and the letter sent by its author, Brenda Anderson, from her home, Vinlandia, in Newport, Rhode Island. Sigurlína took her time with the writing because she didn't want to set the delivery aside; she wanted to look at the letter and the manuscript, yet it wasn't possible to do so—Hoffmann had a unique way of constantly monitoring her, even when he was immersed in his work. And just then, without looking up, he stretched out his hand and asked for the package's contents. Sigurlína continued with her pile as she watched her master beside her. He read the letter and began to leaf through the manuscript. He started to read it. Every now and then he took a deep breath, but finally he put down the papers, leaned back in his chair, and stroked his palm and slender, long fingers across his face. It was almost more physical expression than he had shown when she appeared on his doorstep about two weeks ago.

The next evening, she was hemming her skirt. Outside the window, a horse neighed. Then the big door slammed shut again. She ran to the window, made a small slit in the thick curtains and saw Hoffmann getting into his carriage. Where was he going? He wasn't in the habit of leaving the house at night. She continued with the hem. Who was Brenda? Vinlandia? She put down her sewing. She thought about going downstairs. Only to check if the manuscript was still there. She knew she probably wasn't allowed to be in the room alone at night, but it wouldn't take long. And before she knew it, she was standing in the library, in front of the big desk. Looking right at the manuscript. The letter from Brenda on top of the book. She looked at it as quickly as possible: a short, polite request that Hoffmann read her manuscript. A thank you for Hoffmann's research into what Brenda called "an important part of our history." Now Sigurlína started reading the manuscript herself; she didn't look up as she took a seat in her master's chair. It seemed to be some kind of biography of Guðríður Þorbjarnardóttir, based on the Vinland sagas, and not very accurately, with a number of additions. Pretty inspirational, actually—Sigurlína didn't quite know what to think. But she couldn't stop reading, couldn't break away from the exciting scenarios and descriptions, the fabricated conversations and strong passions. She read about Einar Þorgeirsson's arrival at Arnarstapi, his gifts to Guðríður, a belt with a gold tip: "For you, my lady, if you will accept it." She read about their love affair and its end, the family's sailing to Greenland, the prophecy of Þorbjörg the Little Sybil, Þorsteinn and Guðríður's wedding, Þorsteinn's death—but just as Karlsefni entered the scene, Sigurlína jumped at loud hoofbeats. Hoffmann! She shook the stack of papers together, laid it on the table, and replaced the letter from Brenda on top. Then she turned off the light and ran toward the door. Right then, she heard the front door slam shut.

She has her hand on the doorknob, unable to decide whether to try to rush out and upstairs or to wait, hoping Hoffmann will go straight up to his room without stopping in the library. But as soon as she makes her decision, he's standing in the doorway and she runs right into his arms. He remains immobile, not trying to prevent her from leaving, but simply, in his state of upset, not moving aside. A few moments of this impasse make it seem like it will last forever, neither of them uttering a word, neither of them able to stir, until Sigurlína edges very carefully around the man. Her forehead brushes his damp beard, and the shiver that runs through her body is not a chill but a sensation that grips her as he takes her arm, forcing her to look up, straight into his eyes. Bright and terrifying, terrifyingly beautiful, really, until he closes them and wraps his arms around her. His embrace is firm, his arms smell of exotic scents. Feeling so much contact after her long and strange loneliness in this big house, in this big city, is almost impossible for her, but she doesn't want the feeling to pass, so she wraps her thin arms around his waist and presses her face up to his chest. She closes her eyes and digs deeper into his midst—but then suddenly he lets go, almost pushes her away. He has been addressed. Mr. Gilbert has come into the hall to attend to his master and to take care of his other needs, according to the house's customs and traditions, and in the act, which ends with Hoffmann disappearing into his library, it's as if Sigurlína evaporates. She somehow makes it upstairs to her room, where she comes to her senses and finds the incident too strange to have actually taken place, but the dampness that still clings to her forehead and the pouring rain outside the window indicate that the moment wasn't imagined. But what happened? She had felt the closeness she longed to feel, peering into the mystery of this man. "But what was he thinking?" she wondered as she undressed. Were his intentions romantic? She had never looked at him like that before. It was downright ridiculous to think so! How was she supposed to greet him the next day?

But all her worries were unnecessary, because when Hoffmann had closed the door behind him, tipsy and confused by his incomprehensible reaction to this child-like, bright woman from Iceland, tormented by the thought of his unbridled and lustful behavior in Madame Chapman's house earlier in the evening, he ran up the stairs to the balcony, grabbed the high ladder that stood there on the platform and pushed it toward the bookshelves, hurling himself up to the highest step, where he thought he would find what he was looking for, leaning back so he could read the golden letters on the red spine, losing his balance, falling off the ladder, straight down toward the balcony railing.

Franz W. Hoffmann gave a very low scream. The fresco shone down on him, the image of the goddess Holda grasping a tree branch in one hand, a spool of yarn in the other, spinning the thread, naked underneath her long, blonde hair. Why had the artist chosen this particular story to paint right here inside his temple? He had never understood it, nor did he understand it now, even as he looked at the picture from the point of view of a man seesawing on the railing before falling down to the hard, cold, stone floor. Sigurlína awoke from the confusion of her thoughts. A weighty thump. Shortly afterward, a girl could be heard shouting. Then dead silence. Under Mr. Gilbert's unerring direction, the disaster was smoothly handled. Almost as if the people had expected their master's end was around the corner.

Sigurlína doesn't really hear what the man sitting in front of her is saying; she forgot his name as soon as he introduced himself. He's a young man but very self-assured, resembling the historian Bogi Melsteð, she thinks. He's the estate manager. Hoffmann's library is going to be moved in its entirety, to an institution named after him, but the house and other properties will be sold off to fund the library's future needs. The people in the house will be relocated, ensuring their secure future, per the will of the deceased. Sigurlína's position, however, is unclear; she is not mentioned by name in his will. Is she his scribe? Some kind of Icelandic assistant? "Oh, dear me!" The estate manager is afraid it will be difficult to find her another comparable job in the city—and he obviously finds some amusement in the situation—although there is certainly enough work to be had here, not least for a secretary. But there's a snag, which still seems to make this American Melsteð smile: English is not her mother tongue. Does she know anything besides Icelandic? The young man lights himself a cigar, as if giving Sigurlína time to think about where her talents lie. He gets no answer until after he has blown the smoke out between his wide lips and repeated his question.

Sewing. She says she knows how to sew. The man reacts with immediate delight and tells her that her prospects are assured! Here in the city, sewing takes place in every nook and cranny. He will see to it that she gets a job in that field, and in all fairness—though he is of course not obliged to do so—he will provide her with housing for the time being.

The next day, a carriage waits outside Burgdorf. The trunk is in the lobby, but Sigurlína is inside the library, where the estate manager is about to formally evict her from the house. He has not himself found her a position but placed her in a room far down on Waverly Place, with Mrs. Clark. She will make sure Sigurlína gets a sewing job. Then he takes one folded sheet of paper from Hoffmann's desk and writes down the information. Sigurlína puts the instructions in her bag and takes the outstretched, clammy hand of the man who thanks her on behalf of Hoffmann.

The carriage rattles away. Sigurlína is not sure if the feeling is longing or pure disappointment, but she tries to reassure herself that the continuation of this cohabitation would have been too much for her. Now a normal, suitable life awaits her, communicating with living people closer to her own age, a proper connection to the big city. That's how she holds her head high sitting inside the cold, damp carriage, unaware her journey is now headed into the mess of human existence that is the lower part of the city. To where her talents with golden thread and needle have little value. To where Sigurlína from Iceland will no longer be.

III

Werner & Sons

Sigurlína was seventeen years old when she acquired her first sewing machine, a steel machine with a foot pedal, Singer Model 13. Her father had bought it used from the estate of a Danish widow in Eyrarbakki, a purchase somehow connected to moving the estate's library to Reykjavík. And on this machine Sigurlína had sewn quite a few garments for townspeople for a fee, and for her father and brother, but the last garment out of her home workshop was the short black jacket that she wore on her way abroad from Iceland.

The machine Sigurlína sits at now is not dissimilar to the old Singer, sewing in the same fashion, but much faster, with the vibrating shuttle in a small engine compartment, driven by power that runs, via a drive shift, from an electric motor lying under the full-length table, operated by pressing her neat foot, in her new leather-soled shoes, on the pedal. The electricity travels a long way: there are without a doubt three hundred sewing machines in this large hall and just as many girls dressed the same way as Sigurlína, in dark blue aprons. Each of them with their particular work, performing repetitive movements. Sigurlína and her seat-mates at the long table are sewing legs for undergarments out of a pile of material in front of them, material which constantly accumulates because the large man standing in the corner at the back of the hall, the man with the knife, is unstoppable; he cuts through a thick layer of white linen, working from a brown paper pattern, with incredible certainty and skill. No wonder he gets paid many times more for this work than the sea of women filling the hall, more than any of the folders, buttonholers, pressers, lace-makers, and all those who handle the material Sigurlína and friends sew together.

And thus the machines run ten hours a day, six days a week at the Werner & Sons underwear factory, on the top floor of a five-story brick building on Wooster Street, near the foot of Manhattan. A thousand pairs of pants or thereabouts are sewn each day, making the air heavy with material, the noise in the machines enervating, the presence of foremen and superiors unbearable. A never-ending shouting and crying out, with no one allowed to lose her grip. During the lunch break, chattering springs up, twittering in foreign tongues. Her dining companions came here from Ukraine, and when they finally spoke to her in a few English words, she discovered they had not come to America in search of adventure or fame. Dina, Marina, and Irina came here with their mother and worked for money they sent back to their village. To their mother's elderly parents. They told her stories of riots, of hunger, of tragedy back home, stories which at times sounded strange in Sigurlína's ears because the girls' expressions were somewhat unaffected and seemed free of all pain. In fact, a lot of what they said sounded a bit like a fiction. For instance, one evening a long time ago, a group of farmers and some villagers stormed their pub, went berserk, and shouted: "Down with the Jews, they killed our emperor!" Then they cleared out the house, emptied the tavern of all its vodka; their father, the tavern owner, died in the fight while swinging his ax in the air. Then, with a sudden smile, the sisters wanted to know something about her. Where was she from? No, they had never heard of Iceland, and then it was as though Sigurlína had never heard of Iceland either, because when she thought of her little village she had no words to describe it. Reykjavík was like nowhere else, but it was in no way unique. Just small. There were many mountains in Iceland, and majestic waterfalls. The sisters stopped smiling and asked why she had come to sew here in the city. Did she have relatives here? No, came here on her own, she came to see the world. Laughter pealed from the next table and at that same moment Jacob the foreman shouted over the group, signaling work must begin again. Jacob: a short, dainty young man with raven-black hair.

Sigurlína looked down at the white linen, how it flowed almost automatically under the machine's presser foot, the same movement over and over again. One leg of underwear after another. Worldliness? Hardly. And she did feel a little smug, when she thought of the three girls, her co-workers.

It was Saturday, and they all had envelopes of money in their bags. They went into the cloakroom together, walked down the four flights of stairs and out into the street. There they parted, Sigurlína heading north and the Ukrainian trio east toward Hester Street, where they lived with their relatives. Once home, they continued to sew, fashioning flowers on hats, sundry stuff. Sewing well into evening.

Sigurlína turned right onto Bleecker Street, and then walked up along Broadway to East 9th Street. There she turned right again, onto 4th Avenue: *Cheapest Bookstore in the World*. She had been there several times to look at books under the watchful eyes of the bad-tempered bookseller. She was not looking for anything in particular, just something cheap to shorten her time alone at night. There were a lot of novels. She loitered in front of the shelves, looked and read. Many tempting titles.

"Five cents!" The bookseller had lost his patience and was now standing in front of Sigurlína with a booklet in his hand. She was so alarmed that she immediately reached into her bag to pay the man for the little book and then took the most direct route out of the store. At the next street corner, she stopped: *Nick Carter Arrested by Mistake*. A serial detective story. On the cover was a picture of two men storming into a train car with pistols in their hands. They were pointing them at two passengers. Two women in the front of the carriage looked on in horror. Sigurlína put the pamphlet in her bag and continued downstairs. It was not a lot of money, but she would have rather spent it at the baker on the corner of East 8th Street, she thought, as she headed down to Waverly, toward the house of the old widow Mrs. Clark, where she had a small room, paid for by Hoffmann's estate. Mrs. Clark was a friendly woman who had introduced Sigurlína to Hans Werner, the factory owner, sending her down there with a note on a slip of paper, a pointless recommendation on behalf of "Sewlína" so that she could become the millionth factory girl in Manhattan. Back when she revealed her sewing talents to the cheerful, American Melsteð behind the cigar smoke inside Hoffmann's office two weeks prior,

Sigurlína had had no idea sewing could conjure up the image she was now a part of.

Six dollars. Only one third what she'd earned a week with Hoffmann, but still considered good. She put the bills in her small wooden chest, under assorted papers and photographs. After two weeks, Clark would charge her for the room and food, and what would be left of her salary would be scarcely more than three dollars a week. The fare all the way to Iceland cost maybe forty dollars, so it was touch and go if she would make it home this spring. She closed her chest and set it back in place, under the blanket at the foot of the iron bed. The bed, moderately firm, stood along the wall under two windows that looked out onto the street. Next to the bed was a high table with a jug of water and a bowl, but above the table hung a mirror, so small it only just fit her face. At the end of the bed stood her old trunk, and next to it a desk and a chair. The toilet was out in the corridor.

Sigurlína had gotten into bed and had just opened the Detective Carter novel when she heard people talking outside the window. She got up and carefully slid the window up a short way. She was trying to see if it was the young man in the basement who sometimes stood outside the house smoking cigarettes; he would smile at her when she came home at night. As soon as she stuck her head through the window opening, the two men stopped talking. One of them was her neighbor. He looked up. They both looked up, and from their reaction it was clear they weren't happy being observed, so Sigurlína pulled her head back in and closed the window.

She went back to bed and started reading but couldn't focus on the story. How had the Russian Emperor been overthrown? Had her girlfriends from the factory witnessed their father being killed swinging his ax? She sat up and reached for her wooden box. Underneath a thin woolen rag lay three photographs. One, framed, the picture of her mother; a second, her Confirmation picture; the third—she did not know what to make of it now—a picture of Jón, taken in Copenhagen. Splendid but a little distressed, one hand on a pedestal, wearing a made-to-measure overcoat and with a dark bow around the high collar that looked snow-white compared to the tan, lean face. In the box, among some old newspaper clippings, she had put the sixteen dollars she had saved up, as well as some old letters, one from her loving mother to Laughing Lína, who was reading and studying with her aunt up north in Akureyri. Such a strong sentiment from a single hand. Sometimes she felt she sensed her mother more strongly by looking at her handwriting than her face in a photograph. She gently traced her fingers over the characters before carefully inserting the letter and the dollars into a copy of an old article from the newspaper *Þjóðólfur*, "Women in America."

Sigurlína gasped for breath, hands outstretched trying to help the wounded man.

Dina said she was sixteen, but Sigurlína felt sure she was just a child. She worked quickly but impatiently, and sometimes the foreman, Jacob, shamed her for her skewed sewing; when he turned away from her, she would retort in some foreign words that led to a scolding from her sisters.

And one Monday things were about to reach a boiling point inside the sweatshop on Wooster Street: there were fewer people in the cavernous room than usual, and the piles of material by the machines on the long table kept heaping higher as Jacob ran light-footed and almost insane between stations, making an ear-piercing sound. Dina was tired and constantly coughing, and although she kept up her work it wasn't in line with the demands of Werner & Sons under-garment factory. The perfect climate for disaster hung in the air and just before the lunch break, it happened: Dina sneezed so violently she wrenched the linen from its track right as Jacob happened to be standing directly behind her. He was clearly having a bad day, and he let Dina know it.

His voice was sharp, almost furious. But this was not Dina's day either: once he finished his angry rant, the young girl rose from her seat and left the table. Her sisters could hardly look up from their work, but Sigurlína gently eased her foot off the pedal and watched the girl walk briskly along the hall with Jacob at her heels, saw him grab her and try to pull her back to her seat. More and more girls looked up from their machines to observe the foreman's actions and Dina's reaction. Their interaction was about to turn into some kind of fight; Dina was not going to give up, so Jacob tightened his grip. Sigurlína was standing now, and when Dina began to whine, more weakly than her assertive voice, she ran toward them. She did not know what she was going to do, but involuntarily grabbed Dina's upper arm to free her from the foreman's clutches. As she was about to pull the girl toward her, Jacob shouted so loudly and terribly that all his previous shouting and crying out during difficult factory days was like a pitiful mewling in comparison. And as soon as he screamed, Dina fell into Sigurlína's arms, but broke free at once, ran toward the stairs, and hurled herself down them. Everyone's eyes were on Sigurlína and the foreman, who had stopped screaming and now just stood stiffly and looked at his outstretched hand as if he were examining a thing he had never seen before. And he probably never had seen his hand in this condition before: bloody and swollen after a human bite. Sigurlína flailed in the air, hands outstretched trying to help the wounded man. But he didn't care for help, just pushed her away with his bloodied hand. In came the factory owner, one of Werner's sons. And it didn't take long for him to put two and two together, the bloody hand of the moaning foreman and Sigurlína standing, staring in front of him.

Jacob had been given some canvas off-cuts by the cutter, who was inspecting the wound while Werner's son signaled that Sigurlína should follow him into his office. Jacob was in too much pain to make any attempt to correct the terrible misunderstanding. Nor did any of the women who witnessed the events: recent days in the factory had taught them that it didn't pay to take care of what didn't fall within their purview. Someone had to answer for the act, and Sigurlína herself was hesitant to deny this offense, given a child had committed it. After all, she didn't have any sense of the punishment awaiting her. Indeed, she could barely think straight as she sat inside the factory owner's office with her coat and hat on. When she was finally collected, she didn't say a word. She left the building accompanied by a police officer.

It had snowed a little. She couldn't quite remember how she got here. The policeman had led her out of the factory building into the street and from there into an alley and along various passageways hidden behind the streets. Everything was full of filth and rubbish, and in some places they had to slip past laundry that hung across the passage. Scattered street-urchins here and there, and by the time they returned to the main streets, the children had come together to shout at this girl who had clearly been arrested. And so she disappeared inside her head, thinking of cranesbills and chamomile, of summer sun on the hillside behind their farm. She had sensed a long-forgotten smell, a lost image of her mother, her mother's sunbaked face and golden hair against the green grass. Bursting out laughing, lifting her small child up in the air above her. When the sturdy net of iron bars crashed closed, Sigurlína felt a cold gust rush toward her. And then it went dark.

The night passed in tumult and scuffles. Thieves and murderers, all sorts of jailbirds and bandits competing to raise their objections, prostitutes screaming and begging for clemency ending in cold, loud laughter, in profanity and ugly words. Then everything fell quiet. Until someone started crying. Low, anguished. The crying seemed to come from inside the wall, through a tiny hole on which Sigurlína had fixed her eyes as she sat trembling on the bare iron bunk. What if she were sent to be examined, adjudged to be mentally ill? Women have been deemed cracked for less than biting people and drawing blood. Exiled to an island, to an asylum where they are undressed, scrubbed in ice-cold water, fed rotten food, surrounded by rats and other creatures, kept handcuffed, beaten into obedience until they finally lose their minds, justifying their treatment.

"Miss." Sigurlína didn't hear the prison guard address her, so he put his hand on her shoulder and shook her gently. It was morning and they walked along a long corridor and from there into a large room. There was a smattering of anxious people on the benches but the prisoners waited in line to be called before the police court. After Sigurlína had repeated her name twice, the judge asked after her background. She told him; he uttered a confused response then asked her how long she had lived in America. She said she had been here almost two months. Could she explain what happened at her workplace yesterday? Sigurlína looked down and pleaded not guilty to all the violence. She had only intended to intervene in a conflict that had arisen due to the workload. "My dear child." The judge looked her straight in the eye and said she probably could not return to Werner & Sons. Did she have any resources? Did she have relatives in the city? Where was she living? Then he gave her a scolding and directed her out of the building.

She had escaped with a warning, and once she was out on the street she started running for fear justice would change its mind. But Sigurlína was not herself; she ran south and lost her bearings for a while. Then she turned around, followed Bowery up to Grand Street. And there, it hit her that she had not eaten for more than a day. She decided to stop by the bakery and buy a cake. "Bombolone!" The baker shouted when Sigurlína pointed to a sugar-coated bun in one of the mountains of sweets inside Ferrara.

She was back on Bleecker Street. The sun had warmed the air and dried the streets. It was a beautiful day, and when Sigurlína thought of Mrs. Clark's room, her bed, and her belongings, she began to cry. She wiped her face, her mouth full of the baker's goodness, and continued on. As she approached Waverly Place, she noticed the streets were wet again. It was as though the heavens had only rained here and as she turned the corner, she stepped into a puddle and almost tripped over a thick hose lying across the sidewalk. She looked up. The street was full of people, a strange silence hung in the air. There were policemen and men with big hats. Firefighters. People milled about the wet ground looking up at a building, a black concrete frame behind a thin cloud of smoke. There had been a fire which had been put out. It was Mrs. Clark's house. Sigurlína moved closer, joining the silent throng.

She did not know how long she stood there, but the watching people had left, as had the fire brigade. No one remained but a handful of policemen. One of them was posted at the entrance of the house and she found herself walking toward him. She said her name was Sigurlína Brandsson and that she lived here. What had happened to Mrs. Clark? She needed to get inside. The police officer took her by the hand, said that the occupants of the house had been taken to the hospital, Mrs. Clark too—dead of smoke inhalation. Sigurlína broke free, saying she had to enter. The man replied that it wasn't safe but Sigurlína struck him when he tried to stop her. He chased her into the house but stopped at the first step of the stairs; by then, she had already reached the second floor. He called up to her.

The door to her room is standing ajar. The ceiling saturated, the floor covered in wet ashes, the furniture too, her trunk. She pushes what's left of the lid open. Everything is layered in soot, the books crumble in her hands, the clothes useless: her Sunday dress, the ballgown, the jacket, her straw boater, her undergarment. All that's left is the bed, its iron frame. The blanket and the mattress have burnt up entirely but at the foot of the bed she can make out the outlines of her small wooden box. It had burned happily. The lid curled in half. The glass in the picture frame is cracked, her mother's picture gone black; she cannot recognize her own face in her Confirmation photograph; Jón falls to pieces in her hands. Letters and other papers ruined by water and soot, her banknotes worthless. Everything gone except one thing. A thing that does not really belong to her but has ended up in her possession. It's lying there underneath everything. Carbon black but whole: the old cape clasp. The brooch.

Sigurlína sits on the bed. She takes off her hat and lies down. The black, sodden remnants of the mattress yield to the weight of her body so that the iron coils thrust into her gaunt flesh and the light hair loosely tied at the nape of her neck. But she does not feel them, just overwhelming fatigue. Nothing can be felt except an uncontrollable desire to fall asleep. And she closes her eyes and is about to do so when the policeman shouts once again: "Miss Branson, Miss Branson! Selena?"

IV

Carlson's Curiosity Shop

She had gone up the slope again, rolling down the grass with her mother in the scorching sun, but was suddenly at the farm. As a young girl, dressed in a gown, standing up against a white sheet that the photographer had strung up over the farm's wall. She seemed a little nervous, as if she were being sent to the moon, but her sense of anticipation was stronger, her excitement at becoming a moment that would get preserved forever. But when it finally happened, it was as if she was somewhere else. As if she had simply evaporated. Everything went white, fantastically bright, so that she was forced to close her eyes. And when she opened them again, she could see only black. Her back ached. Her nose and mouth were full of ash. The air was cold and damp. She got up. Selena.

She walked slowly down the stairs, stepping cautiously on each blackened step. She felt the cold wind all around. When she went outside, the policeman was nowhere to be seen; everyone had left. She stood on the sidewalk, inert. For a moment she thought of falling to the ground, throwing herself into the street, because there was no way out. But she could neither fall down nor stand still so she walked on, hesitantly and in various directions alternately. Gradually, she began to realize where she was headed. She was going down to Wooster Street, to the Werner & Sons factory. She was going to put her house in order. She had no other choice.

She stood in front of the building and shuffled her feet once again. Something at the end of yesterday's situation, her horrible arrest, made her hesitant. The shame, certainly. And she was angry and thought it was both unfair and ridiculous. But as she was deep in thought, she saw a man came out of the building. She recognized him immediately. It was the presser. She ran toward him and met a forced smile. It was clear that he knew what had happened. He looked down and grew serious as he tried to explain to her that if she was going in, she would have to prove her innocence. And she could only do that by pointing the finger at little Dina, who had returned to work as if nothing had happened; it had clearly been agreed who was to blame in the case.

Sigurlína was furious but then realized how hopeless her position was. She told the presser about the fire in her landlord's house, that she did not know a single soul in the city, that she only had thirty cents in her purse. Then, finally, he looked into her eyes and she could see he felt sympathy for her, that hers was in so many ways an incredible and cruel fate. However, he said he could offer her nothing but sending her down to Hester Street. There she would not have to wander about for long until someone offered her work, and perhaps she could even get housing with an employer.

The presser had to hurry off so there was nothing for Sigurlína to do but leave before evening fell. She was just around the corner from Bowery, approaching the most densely populated urban area in the world, where more than a thousand people lived in a single hectare. She couldn't work out for certain which way to go, going first right and then left. She circled in the middle of an ocean of people; for a while, she didn't even know where she was. It was getting dark and she was calling on God. Then he stood there in front of her. Had he read the despair in her water-blue eyes? Nothing else directly indicated she was a woman in need, wearing her new—albeit sooty—coat, and a large hat on her head. She extended her hand and cried out for help. Rubinov looked at her through black eyes: Was she lost? Where had she come from? Did she need a job? Maybe also shelter? She didn't say a word, just nodded, because he seemed kind enough and was more or less well dressed.

They walked down the street, she following him. She walked alongside him; it felt good to find herself doing so. To be on her way somewhere. And the path lay through an even greater throng. Suddenly the air was filled with incomprehensible noises and shouts, with arresting signage written in unfamiliar characters, with men walking the streets with big beards, wearing long black coats and kashkets.

Now the two of them were in an unkempt alley and their path led through a narrow door. Up the stairs and into a blackness that smelled of food. Fish? Onions? Cabbage? Sigurlína could not be sure but she felt the air get denser as they ascended. On the top floor they went down a long corridor, and at the end a door opened onto the man's home; as they entered, it seemed to be some kind of workshop. Sigurlína looked around and thought that even though the Reykjavík cottages were poor, their condition was somehow a natural, integral element in the townspeople's primitive, simple way of life, whereas here the homes were like ghosts from the past, their condition a reminder of destruction or decline. Degradation. Congestion. Clutter. The man's living quarters amounted to little more than a large living room filled with tables, several sewing machines, and reams of fabric. She was directed to a corner at the end of the room, a piece of wood set between the walls with something akin to a thin mattress on top of it. It was all torn up and filthy, but under the plank of wood were blankets, as if someone slept there, too. Sigurlína was so disgusted with the mess that, had she not been so dead on her feet, and the pregnant Rubinova not so kind when she pointed her to this wretched situation, she would no doubt have fled this lair, taking the most direct route possible out of there.

Of course she couldn't fall asleep. She lay there in her clothes, on the mattress, on top of the plank, her cape spread over her. Nothing under her head. Her purse beside her, her hat on top of her purse. Had she managed to end up destitute? What misfortune was she living through? And where was she supposed to attend to her own hygiene, where was she supposed to get a nightgown, a shirt, something to change into? "Underwear!" What a fate. Could she wait for the three dollars Rubinov planned to pay her for the week? A whole week. Sigurlína didn't think it was likely she would last the night.

From inside the darkness, the sounds of snoring. And such a stench. She pulled the coat up over her head. It was almost like sleeping outside. What was she doing here? She had to get away. Could she sell her hat to pay for somewhere nicer to rest her head? How many nights would it fetch her? Sigurlína squeezed her eyelids tight, and, little by little, it appeared to her. She crawled out from beneath her coat, delved into her purse, and took out the brooch. Carbon black, black as darkness. She began to rub it against the mattress, then her skirt, working furiously at it. The metal came to glisten, even, she thought, to illuminate her nook under the sloped ceiling, this evil little thing that she had not been able to rid herself of, refusing to disappear from her life. But now it would be her savior. She set the brooch on her chest and was deep in her thoughts; she walked up Broadway to Waverly and, just before she ran out of steam, reached 11th Street. And there it hung before her, the sign: *Carlson's Curiosity Shop*.

She startled when she saw her face in the glass. Frightfully tired under her ridiculously large hat, though her eyes shone with determination. A strange combination, one she herself hardly recognized, but when she moved closer to the window, her face disappeared and she saw a curved sword and a pistol, a musket and a rifle, a badge of honor, a metal horn, a lone spur, and an epaulette. The items were from the Civil War, but the shop window also displayed other exhibits: a wooden statue, a painting of a man with a lute, various kinds of embroidery, a walking stick with ivory handles, two porcelain plates, a gold-plated mantel clock, a pile of yellow papers and a few parchment books.

She closed the door behind her. If the window display was chaotic, there was no good way to describe what confronted her inside. Given the enormous quantity, all that stuff could hardly be worth much of anything. She was standing in a kind of corridor, on either side of which were walls of merchandise, stacked floor to ceiling. At the end of the corridor was a spiral staircase to the store's upper level where there was even more junk. She called out a good morning but got no response so she decided to head up. And there he sat at his desk, the gray-haired Carlson, a short, old man, a little like she had imagined him, but more friendly than she had expected. In a thin voice he asked how he could assist her and offered her a seat. She shuffled past and clambered over wooden junk, papers, and armor to get to the table.

Sigurlína took the cape clasp from her bag, laid it on the table and asked for its value, though she did not specify whether she was pawning it or offering for sale, because just at this moment she was not sure. She said the clasp had been found buried in Iceland. That it was a thousand years old. Carlson examined it with hand gestures and grimaces, picked up the object and moved it about under his magnifying glass. "Twenty dollars," he pronounced, laying the brooch on the table and folding his arms as a sign that it was his final offer.

Twenty dollars? It was almost what she had paid for her coat and hat. Watson could hardly have snatched something so insignificant. And if Carlson had bought the clasp, the seller—Sigurlína pushed away the thought that the seller even existed—would have needed more for his effort alone. The brooch must be more valuable than that, even if only for the fragments of gold in the frame. And, anyway, twenty dollars would not rescue her except for a moment from the hell that her existence in the city had become.

She took the brooch off the table, put it in her bag, stood up, and politely expressed her gratitude. Carlson also stood up, trying to explain to her that the item didn't seem to be of much value, that he had no proof that it was so old. For that, he needed more knowledge of its material and pattern. But Sigurlína was already on her way out, clambering over the junk on the floor again and going confidently down the stairs. Carlson went after her and called down from the top step that maybe he was not the right buyer for her find. It would be better to take it to an antique auction that took place from time to time here in the city.

From time to time? That wouldn't work, given her situation, so she took hold of the doorknob and said goodbye for the second time. But just before she stepped out, he called after her that another option was to take the brooch to the museum. The Metropolitan Museum. There she should at least be able to have its value accurately assessed.

She paused in the doorway and pondered the old man's words for a moment—but had to rush if she was to get back in acceptable time. She walked fast, almost running at times, looking neither right nor left, talking to herself loud enough that everyone could hear even though no one was listening. How had she thought about doing such a thing? Selling what she did not own! Making money from a theft. Sell it? No, not exactly.

Sigurlína was still in the midst of her conversation when she walked into Rubinov's. He wasn't too happy about the sudden disappearance of his new employee, but she didn't care, just sat down at her table and continued with the neckwear from the morning so she would get her bread, coffee and sauerkraut, a shelter in a peculiar place and a disgusting mattress to sleep on. Besides herself, there were three women working in the sweatshop, all a little older than herself, and a man with a pressing iron. Some children seemed to have a minor role there too. But she paid little attention to it all, so preoccupied was she with easing her conscience, steeling herself, filling her head with accusations against other people until her face was almost disfigured.

That evening, she crawled into her nook for the second time, squeezing into a worn but fairly clean nightdress Rubinova had given her. She lay awake a long time, listening to strange, coarse voices within the darkness. She opened her purse and drew out the new notebook she had bought with her wages from Werner & Sons. She had still not yet mustered the energy to put her name in it. She found her pencil stub. And using her new name, Selena Branson, she was inspired to make mad, mischievous plans until she was fast asleep.

She let the precious object drop into her handbag.
Then she ripped out the first pages of the detective story
from the loose spine and carefully wiped herself.

They: the ten board members seated around a table inside the
meeting room of the Metropolitan Museum, a moderately
magnificent Gothic-style brick building inside Central Park,
its south entrance, overlooking the city's reservoir. A rather
dilapidated area. The men are: Cornelius Vanderbilt, who,
with his election to the board, brought the museum numerous drawings by da Vinci, Michelangelo, and Raphael, as well
as one of the museum's most popular paintings, *The Horse
Fair,* by the French artist Rosa Bonheur, which he bought
at auction for fifty-three thousand dollars in 1887; Edward
Dean Adams, the president of Niagara Falls Hydraulic Power and Manufactuing Company, numismatist and collector
of bronzes; Samuel P. Avery, art dealer; John Bigelow, author
and former American ambassador to France; Heber R. Bishop, businessman and owner of the greatest collection of jade
in America; James A. Garland, railroad baron and owner of
all the Chinese porcelain preserved in the museum; John S.

Kennedy, an investor and art collector who recently donated to the collection a twenty-five-square-meter canvas by Emanuel Leutzes, *Washington Crossing the Delaware*; John Pierpont Morgan, one of the most powerful men in the American financial world and a collector of all kinds—in addition to a huge library of books and works of art, he is the owner of a valuable gem collection and the largest collection of medieval artifacts in America; Joseph H. Choate, a jurist and one of the founders of the museum, and whose policy was to reject the distinction between fine arts and historical treasures, holistically collecting art and antiquities from the beginning of history to the present era in order to inspire and guide the masses. Finally, the chairman himself, Henry G. Marquand, a wealthy and very discriminating art collector. It's he who gave the museum *Young Woman with a Water Pitcher*, the first of Dutch painter Johannes Vermeer's works purchased for an American collection—the very painting Sigurlína, cold and wet after a long walk in pouring rain all the way from Ludlow Street, was now staring at as it hung against a red wall on the museum's upper floor. She was waiting for the board meeting to end so she could meet the eleventh man at the table, the director of the Metropolitan Museum, the Italian-born Luigi Palma de Cesnola. She had taken a seat on a hard wooden bench in the middle of the floor and was listening to water drip through the roof and down into two pails at her feet. Her handbag was in her lap, her right hand on her bloated belly.

Sigurlína was in pain. A young man sat down on the bench next to her, grabbed a large piece of bread from his soot-black coat, and began to tear into it, causing breadcrumbs to fly all over the place. Sigurlína stood up and went into the next room, past Chinese jars, plates and dragons;

she turned left and was back inside the room hanging with paintings. A young woman stood before one of them, leaned her torso across a gilt barrier that was bolted to the floor, extended her hand and placed it on the surface of the image: a lady in a flowing smock with a nosegay of violets. Next to her, a parrot perched on a stand. Édouard Manet. The guest stroked her hand down the painting's surface, tugging it to her as the lapdog she was holding started to bark. The woman hurried off, followed by a guard who came rushing from the next room, a room full of ancient fragments and miniscule objects. Glass, silver, and gold from Cyprus. Whole heaps, glittering behind glass in ornate cabinets. True treasures.

But what was this? In front of Sigurlína stood two older women, fiddling with one of the display cabinets. To her, it looked as though they were trying to force open the glass which sealed in the necklaces and assorted gold pieces from the fourth century BC. She let out a choking sound, and at the same moment the women jerked their hands back; the guard, quick on his feet, entered the chamber again, though he didn't get to intervene in what the women were up to because at the same moment, and from the other direction, two young men entered the room, men he needed to escort out when one of them spat tobacco on the floor. They were causing a scene.

Sigurlína went back down to the first floor. More glass cabinets, long rows and tall, with stone statues inside them. She sat down. From all directions they stared at her: white, stately heads from a long-distant past. Her plans seemed nonsensical. But she tried to hold her head high, not leaving here until she had offered the museum the treasure which fate had bequeathed to her. And then for a second time a man sat next to her. Right beside her. Some kind of aristocrat, she imagined, from the look of the gleaming shoes and the stiff-pressed pants; she inhaled the scent of the man's perfume. He crossed his legs and stabbed his staff incessantly against the floor, a walking stick with a knob in the shape of a lion's head. He was counting down and now he swung his stick up and forward to point at a small statue behind the glass. It was a woman made of limestone, dressed in a tunic and sandals, wearing a headband, a chain around her neck, earrings in her ears, and a snake around one arm. Her left hand held onto her garment and a mirror. The man touched his staff lightly against the glass: "Aphrodite?" Then he prattled on about something Sigurlína didn't really follow, tittered, shook his head, pushed his staff against the floor and got up from the bench. He bowed in front of the glass and walked out of the hall, swinging the staff. Sigurlína watched the man disappear into the next room and decided that enough time had passed since she had announced her errand down in the lobby.

The director, Cesnola, referred to himself by the title "General." He was given that designation verbally by Abraham Lincoln just a few days before his assassination. He was subsequently made U.S. Consul in Cyprus, an outpost of the Ottoman Empire. And there, almost overnight, began his unprecedented career as an amateur archeologist and excavator. Without keeping any records of it, he led a group of diggers in an extensive excavation in the ancient settlement of Golgoi, and soon his home in Larnaca was filled with treasures, amassing into thousands. He sold objects here and there, but his dream was to sell the collection as a whole. For a time, it seemed that Napoleon III had the intention to purchase the collection and present it to the Louvre, but those plans came to naught when the Franco-Prussian War broke out in the summer of 1870. Cesnola then corresponded with the State Hermitage Museum in St. Petersburg and the British Museum in London, but in the end the newly founded Metropolitan Museum in New York bought his entire collection, paying sixty thousand dollars for it. That was in 1874.

But it wasn't altogether easy to bring all the artifacts—stored in many hundred wooden chests—out of the country to London en route to New York City: the Grand Vizier in Constantinople tried to stop the export and a part of the collection went into the sea off the coast of Syria. The rest, however—no small collection—reached its final destination, and the Metropolitan paid Cesnola to carry out further excavations in Cyprus, this time near the ancient stronghold of Kourion, and eventually made him the first director of the fledgling museum, then housed in an old residential building on 53rd Street. Under Cesnola's command, the museum began to expand and its membership to swell, and in 1880 a new building was inaugurated on the outskirts of the city, in Central Park. This vigorous, animated man, who began his career as a soldier at the age of fifteen in the war over the unification of Italy, fought with the British in the Crimean War, and eventually served as a colonel in the American Civil War, seemed to have unlimited ambition, and that enchanted the museum's trustees, a powerful crowd of wealthy men who, for some reason, had decided to bet on history and art, things about which they knew relatively little but still very much enjoyed.

In academic circles, however, doubts arose as to this spirited figure, especially after two foreign experts published ar-

ticles arguing that the Cesnola collection—which had done
so much to establish the Metropolitan's reputation and was
generally regarded as a remarkable achievement—was not the
"complete picture" Cesnola asserted in his own writings. These
experts further maintained that the museum had conflated objects from dissimilar periods, and even *created* artifacts by placing together unaffiliated parts belonging to different centuries.
These were serious allegations which were brought before an
investigative committee, leading to front-page headlines and,
eventually, lawsuits. And although Cesnola was acquitted of
all charges, his image was tarnished, and the trustees were di-
vided in their support of him. Specialists considered him an
ignorant dilettante, out of touch with the art worlds in both
his home country and in Europe, a charlatan with little interest in anything other than the Cypriot collection preserved
under his name.

Yet he's still sitting there, fifteen years later. His lorgnettes
rest on his nose above a silver-gray walrus moustache. He gruff-
ly invites an unsuspecting Sigurlína to take a seat, his mind off
in the distance as she delivers her message and sets the brooch
on the large tabletop that lies between them. It had been a trying board meeting, like so many before; although the agenda
concerned the expansive plans for another museum extension
and the magnificent façade that would face Fifth Avenue, the
discussion had once again turned to the problem of the con-
troversial curator. Not so long ago, a worker in filthy overalls
had been thrown out of the museum at Cesnola's direction
and now newspapers were hammering away at their perpet-
ual, popular assertion that the institution was nothing more
than a living room for the rich, that it had no real interest in
educating the people.

But that was not the principal reason Cesnola barely reacted to the dirty Icelandic brooch now lying on the table before him; the museum scarcely attended to its own curation at
that time since bequests streamed in, donations and gifts alike.
Morgan was beginning to piece together his medieval collection, Marquand's extensive art collection would soon end up
in the Metropolitan, John Jacob Astor and his wife had recently donated all their laces, the trustees had used two hundred
thousand dollars to buy art from the estate of the philanthro-
pist Catherine Lorillard Wolfe, and Egyptian antiquities had
piled up ever since the museum began funding excavations
there more than twenty years ago. Moreover, it was not un-
common for people to come in off the street, people like Sigurlína, knocking on doors and trying to get a valuation for
all sorts of things, antiques of uncertain provenance and ob-
scure stories. Cesnola had recently received a letter from an old
woman in the city earnestly inviting him to buy a painting she
claimed had been found in the ruins of Herculaneum under
the ashes of Vesuvius. Sigurlína's story about the discovery of
the Icelandic brooch was not nearly as fanciful but it had little
meaning amid the historical abundance over which the museum presided. Age alone did not grant access to this temple;
in Cesnola's rough palm her offering was worthless because he
knew nothing about Iceland and its history. So he placed the
poor old brooch back down on the table and gently pushed
it toward the young woman with his index finger: "You need
history to turn old gold into priceless treasure."

Right! The General spoke from experience, having been
accused of augmenting an ancient statue for that very purpose,
the purported Aphrodite in the glass case at the front of the
same room where the perfumed fop with the stick had held

his conversation with himself. The story was that Cesnola, or someone in his circle, had snuck the mirror into Aphrodite's hand in order to support the theory that the little limestone represented the goddess of love and beauty. In this way, he'd sought to enhance the excavation's historical significance and increase the collection's worth.

Sigurlína sat still as a statue. She turned her head to one side and then the other before closing her eyes again. Her sole way out of her miserable existence here in the city had been denied—but then it was as though life itself, her body, came to her rescue, and did so by creating new and completely different kinds of worries, worries about what would happen if she could not keep inside the sneeze that was about to rush down her long and slightly turned-up nose, tremoring like a shiver down her delicate frame with the result that blood would spurt full force down her vagina and in such a magnitude that her three skirts would not be able to soak it all in and a puddle would be left on the light green seat. Seeping into the plush and staining it forever into eternity.

She reached for the brooch very carefully and the concentration that movement required of her caused the air in her nose to retreat, she was momentarily saved, she stood up, careful as a decrepit old man, offered a hasty thanks, and hurried to the door, taking chicken steps, never parting her thighs so nothing would slip out onto the floor—and it must surely have been a strange sight from Cesnola's point of view. If, that is, he watched her go, which is unlikely because this care-worn curator had probably begun thinking of something quite apart from the worthless junk of this childlike woman who was now trying to exit the building as soon as possible, out into the sea of people, out to the wet, sticky ground that might swallow up everything that was now starting to leak down from under her skirt.

What a bathetic, abrupt conclusion after so long a preface! And now nothing ahead but the long way back downtown. And the dark was closing in, so Sigurlína started to run. Always running. She ran past mansions, gleaming horse-drawn carriages, top hats, bustling skirts, Jón, the Editor, all dressed up, department stores, petrol-driven cars, police officers, restaurants, streetcars, Blacks, barking dogs, bookmakers, crooks, fruit sellers, street hawkers, all kinds of junk sellers, newspaper boys, a Chinese lady, butchers, food carts, ruffians, thieves, vagrants, tramps, criminals, murderers, beggars, old men, cripples, street children, a child with a child in its arms, many hundred brothels. Synagogues. As she approached Ludlow Street, she decided to take a short cut. She was standing in a narrow side street that seemed to be never ending and now she felt as if she had gone too far. Through an open door she saw people in a peculiar situation: standing behind the condensation on the pane was a naked man; from the skylight came a strange sound, a howling. There was a peculiar smell in the air. She spent a long time going back and forth in the dark until suddenly she was by Rubinov's alley. And before her: the outhouse. She tore open the door, lifted her skirts and sat down on the coarse wooden plank. She badly needed to get water and something to dry herself with. Oh, what a mess! Where was that catalogue, the tome that had been lying here on the wooden boards last night? Sigurlína rummaged in her bag and fished out the detective novel. Nick Carter. She hadn't opened the book for some time, having been preoccupied with all kinds of thoughts and speculation in recent days. But the four pages she had read were both thin and soft, perfect for wiping. But as she got ready to tear them out, a bookmark, a folded sheet of paper, fell to the floor. She bent down and hunted around for it in the mire.

The moon's reflected light shone through the smashed roof of the outhouse: Waverly Place. There it was, the slip of paper the thick-set estate's executor had reached for on Hoffmann's desk so that he could write down Mrs. Clark's address, not realizing what Sigurlína was about to find out: The piece of paper was Hoffmann's stationery. A beginning of a letter, dated the day he died:

> *Burgdorf. Riverside Drive.*
> *October 19th, 1896*
>
> *Dear Miss Anderson,*
> *I have now read through the draft of your book*
> *Gudrid and I will say*

That was it; nothing more. Perhaps Hoffmann had been disturbed mid-sentence, perhaps Mr. Gilbert knocking on the door with a fresh delivery on crackling machine paper? No, Sigurlína thought, more likely something else would have stopped her old master. Hoffmann had simply not had the courage to say what he really thought about this impetuous, sensational story by Miss Brenda Anderson, a story Sigurlína had only managed to read halfway, but which now came vividly back to her.

Someone kicked the door. Someone with an urgent need outside the outhouse. But their distress had no effect on "Selena Branson." She wasn't done. Glued to the seat, that coarse hole down into the dank-smelling darkness, she thought about the words. She closed her eyes, and Hoffmann appeared before her, eyes light and far away. And from where he was, he looked through her, then disappeared as the wooden floor of the chamber began to vibrate under her toes as she tapped her little black shoes on the wooden boards: "You need history to turn old gold into priceless treasure." This time it wasn't General Cesnola speaking but Sigurlína-Selena herself. Reaching into her purse, she took out the brooch. She pressed her finger on the pin that protruded from its back. No needle? For a few seconds, the crush in her head grew so great that she feared it would sunder, then the tension broke, and a smile played across her face. It was that smile which led people to think of her as a girl holding in a smirk, that smile which made men think she was making fun of them. She held the brooch horizontally in front of her. A clasp for a cape? Who had said so? She let the precious object drop into her handbag: "For you, my lady Gudrid." Then she ripped out the first pages of the detective story from the loose spine and carefully wiped herself.

Maggie O'Reilly

She managed to get some water from the bucket in front of the Rubinovs' bedroom, gathered up a few pieces of fabric from the floor and flung herself onto the bed. But although she was almost bent double by the twists and turns of the day, she couldn't fall asleep. In all likelihood she would have to complete her mission while others slept. Through the window at the other end of the sewing room was a light from the street, but first she had to sneak over to Rubinov's desk and swipe a little ink, an envelope and a stamp. She had a pen in her purse.

Sigurlína gently placed Hoffmann's letter on the cutting board under the window, using a blank page at the back of the Nick Carter novel to practice her hand, composing the letter and verifying it fit with Hoffmann's, this single sheet. His writing, which she knew well enough to imitate, was rather small:

Burgdorf. Riverside Drive
October 19th, 1896

Dear Miss Anderson,
I have now read through the draft of your book
Gudrid and I will say

Sigurlína gently dipped her nib into Rubinov's inkwell, stroking it carefully over the absorbent page of the crime story, and took a deep breath as she picked up the thread where Hoffmann had left it

that I much enjoyed reading it. It seems thoroughly researched on all important issues but most importantly Gudrid comes vividly alive through your excellent portrayal of appearance and character, and elaborate description of clothes and jewelry. Indeed a brass belt tip found in the eroded ruins of a medieval farm in the northern part of Iceland, believed to have belonged to Gudrid, recently came into possession of an Icelandic assistant of mine. A piece you would most certainly be interested in.

I wish you all the best as you continue with this very promising work.

Yours faithfully,
Dr. Franz W. Hoffmann

Sigurlína watched the ink dry, pen in trembling hand. She took an envelope from Rubinov's things and tried to stop herself thinking about the fact that its texture and weight differed from the letter; it was not especially convincing as a wrapping for Hoffmann's sophisticated stationery. She folded the page and sealed the envelope. Naturally, she had not forgotten Brenda's address. Then she crawled into her corner, placing the letter in her purse, which she had snuck under her stiff, heavy blanket. But she didn't manage to fall asleep, especially after she realized that the belt Einar Þorgeirsson the jeweler had brought to Guðríður was probably not mentioned in any of the ancient texts of the *Saga of Erik the Red*. The belt was, like so many things in Miss Anderson's story, a pure fabrication.

And so Sigurlína was of two minds when she emerged onto the street the following morning. And still more led her to have second thoughts about the plot she'd only last night thought was so ingenious, sitting there in the outhouse: Just another spur of the moment madness, was it not? In order for the brooch—now, that is, a belt tip—to enter into world history via this letter, the letter's recipient, Brenda, needed to come into contact with the relic's owner, Sigurlína—and how would she do that, given that Sigurlína wasn't, according to the plot, the real correspondent? And, what's more, not only was the letter a fake, but its contents made up. Shouldn't she think this scheme through all the way to its conclusion? No, damn it, she couldn't afford to think about the consequences of her actions at this moment when her life had become nothing but drudgery, day in and day out. And with that certainty, she walked across the street and toward the mailbox.

Yet her assurance did not prove enough for her, because just before she finished crossing the street she stopped. As if someone had pulled her back. As if a giant hand from above had pinched the back of her coat between index finger and thumb, and pulled her up off the ground and shaken her vigorously. It was not just the consequences she had to fear—that her crime would be revealed—but the act itself. Now she stood rigid, her hands by her sides, drawing deep breaths until all the spark was gone from her. She might well have planned this crime in order to nourish her weak hope, but she couldn't actually carry it out.

Back to square one. Back across the street, with heavy, small steps, not caring where she put her feet. And what happened next had been coming for days. With all these walks around the big city, the sole that Mathiesen the Reykjavík cobbler had nailed on her tiny boot had begun to loosen, and now, this cold early December morning, it twisted half off and gave way as she set her foot on a cobble in the middle of the street, causing her, Sigurlína Brandsdóttir, the daughter of Brandur Jónsson from Kot in Skagafjörður, to lose her balance. She threw her hands into the air and the bag with them, the little embroidered purse flying up into the air and then down to the street just before she herself hit the ground.

She lay dazed for a while, trying to get up. There were people going about their business all around her, but no one seemed to notice what had happened. No one except a single bystander. An old woman standing beside a food cart on what you might call a sidewalk, who rushed across the street at high speed toward Sigurlína. The woman was wearing a thick coat with a fur collar, a fur hat on her head; she wasn't carrying a bag. By the time Sigurlína had gathered herself, the woman had already bent down to the street, grabbed the purse, and thrust herself back into the throng. She moved her feet briskly, even as she hobbled, hastening away from the street then slowing as she turned onto the Bowery. She couldn't know that at the very same moment she snatched Sigurlína's sole possessions off the street, Officer Cooke was turning onto Hester Street. He didn't give a moment's thought to Sigurlína, who was lying there, searching for her bag on the dusty earth, because it was Maggie O'Reilly who was uppermost in his mind. Oh, how many times he'd been a hair's breadth from clasping hold of the city's most notorious pickpocket? This time he was determined to succeed. He jostled through the throng in his double-breasted overcoat and strode large strides along the street after the old woman, and when she turned onto Canal Street, he made a move to grab her. He set his big, bent paw on the old woman's shoulder and clasped hold of her; she wheeled violently around to face him. He looked into her dark countenance: cold eyes, a grimacing slit of a mouth set on coarse, gray skin. They stared at each other for a while. O'Reilly, a.k.a. Blue Edie, made no attempt to break free, simply allowing the watch officer to lead her all the way up to Elm Street and into the gaol.

While this journey was underway, Sigurlína was running up and down Hester Street searching for her purse. O'Reilly's artfully swift snatching of the bag had passed her by, but she had begun to suspect a theft. Still, she ran around there like a madwoman and even began crying out. The few who paid her any mind gave her the evil eye, so she came to a halt, standing still on the sidewalk as people traversed the street, to and fro. The longer she stood in that one spot, the more difficult it became to stir herself. Her head was spinning, a storm whirling inside it. She didn't dare move.

Officer Cooke had by now gone the length of Mulberry and was in his headquarters. He sat down at his desk and placed the stolen goods on the table. He looked out the window and sighed. The sea of people, this sticky, cruel chaos. The day's work had not brought him the satisfaction he was expecting; on the contrary, his struggle with the old pickpocket had left him rattled, and somewhat sapped his strength. He reached out for the embroidered bag and turned it out on his desk. A pen nib, a cracked hair comb, a small, paper-thin notebook marked Selena Branson, a pencil stub, a stained handkerchief embroidered with S and B, a fragment from a dime novel, four pennies, and a small metal object, partly gilded. The officer looked at the stuff on the table in front of him and exhaled. Then he lifted the bag as if he wanted to smell the Icelandic flower: *Dryas octopetala*. And that's how he discovered the envelope at the bottom. His melancholy now turned to curiosity. He didn't recognize the recipient's name, but the address piqued his interest and suggested to him that he should mail the letter. But it also raised his hopes of finding the owner of the bag and the bits and bobs that it contained.

V

Vinlandia

The bright white dustcovers are all that illuminate the dark, large living rooms after the door to the studio has been slammed shut. Inside the atelier, however, everything is bathed in orange light. The air is saturated with the scent of roses. A man and woman are talking in half whispers. He is young, dark, wiry, dressed in a light-colored smock. He is a painter and his canvas is a huge stone wall at the end of the room, four meters high, six meters long. His work is almost complete: a Viking ship on a mirror-smooth sea. A man and a woman are standing in the prow: Þorfinnur Karlsefni and his wife Guðríður, wearing a sapphire blue tunic with a gold belt around the middle, on which the artist is about to put the finishing touches. He stands up on the top of a wooden ladder, brings his face close to the wall and draws the gold threads one after the other, wielding the thin brush with great precision. He leans back to better regard the center of the picture. "Perfect!" he whispers to himself, then suddenly releases a loud sound of panic that dies out slowly and calmly as he steps back onto the rung of the ladder and regains his balance. He breathes a sigh of relief then looks back and marvels at the indifference of his employer, the woman lying on the chaise longue in the middle of the room. Hadn't she heard him? Or was it that Miss Brenda, the late Carl Anderson's only daughter, couldn't be bothered to look up from the letter she'd read and which had been lying on the silver tray on the table by her couch since early today?

She's forty. She's unmarried and wallowing in money. However, one wouldn't describe her as a typical upper-class woman spending her days in philanthropic diversions, wrapped up in her peers' social lives: rather, her peculiarity and her shattered dreams have set her apart from the society to which she formally belongs. In fact, Brenda has never wanted to belong to that community, other than to enjoy its attendant benefits. Her life has been an eternal struggle with her roots: Brenda has always been convinced that her parents' wealth negated her dream of becoming a writer by obstructing her political engagement, hindering any chance of meeting radical groups of writers and artists in the city. Deep down, though, she knows this isn't the case, that something else must explain the difficulty she's had getting her stories published, the ones written under names other than her own.

But Brenda had kept to her version of events, and when she turned twenty-five she decided it was high time to get out of the city for her European tour. After months on the continent, she went to England, where she stayed with family friends, and while there she met a young man, a Scottish linguist, who became totally infatuated with this American girl's Nordic roots. She was charmed again by his free-spirited demeanor and affection. She felt she had finally met her bohemian, the man who told her stories of Nordic warriors, of their achievements, loves, and destinies. But as their meetings went on, it became clear that the Scotsman was no bohemian, just an unstable man who got fixated on one topic or another. Indeed, when she told him that there would be no more meetings, he reacted angrily, with violence, before breaking down and begging her not to leave. It was a rather awkward situation, and in the end the master of the house decided to have the Scot carried out of his home. The young man took to hanging around, on the watch for her, so for a while she stopped daring to leave the house; when it came time to go back home to America, Brenda had become a bag of nerves.

But even though this ambassador for the Icelandic sagas had been too much of a reality for Brenda, the Scot had given her just what she needed: inspiration to write and a book entitled *The Norse Discoverer of America: The Vinland Sagas*, which he had handed to her with great ceremony and style, along with some damn nonsense written on the flyleaf, which Brenda tore out and threw into the fire before she left England with Guðríður in her baggage, her future interest and her hero. And here, as she reclined on the couch in her home, Vinlandia, it seemed as if her dream of many years was finally coming true: in one hand she held the blessing of Dr. Hoffmann—oh, that he should have written to her the day he died—and in the other, the letter from Officer Cooke explaining the facts of the situation and asking for help in finding the owner of a purse that held four pennies, a broken comb, a dirty handkerchief, a notebook marked Selena Branson, and a gilded iron object. But Cooke, of course, didn't know the contents of Hoffmann's letter to Brenda, the key to solving the mystery behind the missing handbag: Hoffmann's female Icelandic assistant was meant to have mailed the letter but forgot it in her purse, which she later lost to a pickpocket. And the golden iron object: Guðríður's belt tip, the treasure the assistant never left unattended. Admittedly, there were a few links missing in this story, but it was enough for Brenda to decide upon her first step once she arrived in the city in two days' time with the manuscript for her book about Guðríður, ready for printing. New York City, where she will reside for the winter at her childhood home on 5th Avenue.

Not under any circumstances
could the name have passed her by.

The first step? It didn't occur to her to look for a police officer when she finally managed to stir from her spot to crawl
back to her insalubrious hole. She had, for as long as she
could remember, sewn, for her own benefit and sometimes
for pleasure, but she hadn't been able to imagine how these
simple movements, that work habit, might save her from
complete despair and madness, how good it was to depress
the iron pedal, to feel the needle shuttle up and down, the
material crawl under the presser foot. She felt the vibrations
spread through her cold hands, wearing her coat as the big
storm slipped in through numerous holes in the roof.

She worked like this for a few days until she went to bed
with a fever. Shaking uncontrollably there on the hard pallet,
she listened to Rubinova's screams from inside the couple's
room. Compassion for a sick seamstress who seemed to have
appeared out of nowhere? Non-existent, of course, much less
since the baby was stillborn. Everything revolved around that
terrible trial, naturally, leaving Sigurlína to crawl, drenched

with sweat, to fetch water and what little necessities she needed and could be found. She barely had thoughts, almost nothing save for the notion that her helplessness was complete, her misery total. And one more thing came to mind. It occurred to her that she had finally become as insignificant as her father had predicted: less than nothing. She tried to think further about her father, if she could somehow reach him from here. About her mother she tried to think as little as possible.

Then one morning she opened her eyes, got up, and sat at the machine again. She was still a little weak, even though she had plenty of food and didn't have to work evenings. This strange living situation consisted of little else. The family kept to themselves; Rubinova, who had cared for her the most, was bedridden. Sigurlína picked fabric up off the floor and tried to create something useful to while away the time. She read an old newspaper the landlord had left behind. She read almost every word, which made it last a few days: Kaiser Wilhelm in Germany was planning to strengthen his navy; there was tension in Haiti; the Chinese were handing over a tract of land near Hong Kong to England; Cuban independence was in sight; there'd been a train accident in Warsaw; a former Uruguayan government minister had been exiled; Martin Thorn, the Manhattan barber, had been sentenced and executed by electric chair in Sing Sing Prison. Thorn had been found guilty of, and had admitted to, killing William Guldensuppe, a German masseur. Sigurlína read about the verdict in a case the newspaper called the most brutal crime that had been committed in the city for a long time. But it said nothing about how the murder of Guldensuppe had gripped the city's residents, police, detectives, and journalists since early summer. Nothing, either, about the circus that had started up, with the street rags of Joseph Pulitzer and William Hearst at the forefront, reporting how a lone farmer out on Long Island found a duck pond on his land turned red as fire; how people picking blueberries in Harlem found a pair of legs in a deep ditch; how two boys playing down by the bridge over the East River at 11th Street caught sight of a bulky bag that turned out to be the body of a man. At the water's edge, the arms floated fast beside the torso. So Sigurlína moved on without reflecting on the tragic end of the love triangle between the barber, the masseur, and the masseur's landlord, a woman named Augusta Nack. She read all kinds of local news, some quite incomprehensible. She was reminded that Christmas was almost here, she read reviews of plays, read about the struggle for equality, about city weddings upcoming and recent. She read obituaries and death notices, any number of press releases, news about murders and suicides. Sigurlína read advertisements for European tours, train journeys from London to Paris and from there down to the French Riviera and on to Italy. About hotels in Florence, Venice, and Rome. Announcements seeking employ. And these she read letter by letter: bookkeepers, upholsterers, bartenders, bakers, clerks, scribes, typesetters, cashiers, drivers, doormen, metalworkers, pianists, goldsmiths, carpenters, machinists, bellhops, printers, decorators, painters, salesmen of all kinds. All these people wanting work. Men wanting to enter into service in a private home or as assistants to the elderly, as stewards, masseurs, cooks, various kinds of servants, drivers, coachmen, grooms, gardeners. Women wanting to become attendants, cooks, domestic laundrywomen, house servants, seamstresses, wealthy ladies' companions, assistants, travel companions, German teachers, French teachers, hairdressers, secretaries, typists. She quickly skimmed over sundry information about import and export. And she glanced at a stock trading chart before reaching for the oil lamp and turning the room dark.

The situation left her deadened, her worries not disturbing her sleep, her days passing with no real plans other than trying to get a letter to Iceland to ask for help. That thought, however, wasn't very appealing, so every now and then she would begin to calculate, wondering if she could pull funds together, get better paid in an actual sewing factory. But then she'd need to find some other place to sleep at night. Should she put an advertisement in the newspaper like these ones? Did this narrow alley even have an address at which people could reply to her?

The landlord had come upstairs for a second time. And again Rubinov was not around, gone out somewhere with a half-sewn garment. But this time the man wasn't going to let his tenant go free; he, this big, weighty man, crammed himself onto a too-small stool against the wall on the left side of Sigurlína's table, right there beside it, and started reading the day's paper. From time to time he made a sound, various sounds, sounds that expressed his disapproval for what he read, mostly, then suddenly he burst out laughing so that Sigurlína jumped as she sat at the machine sewing together a coat sleeve from thick, unmanageable fabric. She looked up and stared in his direction, wishing he could feel her unseen gaze, but of course he did not notice anything from behind the huge newspaper that was moving up and down in concert with the merriment the text was causing him. Up and down, then gradually to a standstill as the man's laughter died off. And there it was, looking directly at her on the right corner of the back page. It was as if the letters floated off the page, rose toward her face, and what's more, they were no ordinary letters. Not under any circumstances could the name have passed her by: *Brenda Anderson.* Sigurlína moved her face closer to the newspaper, looking into a decorative frame around an extended advertisement text entitled: "The Icelandic Discoverers of America Five Hundred Years before Columbus. A lecture on the occasion of the publication of the book *Gudrid. The First Caucasian Mother in America.* Held at the Metropolitan Museum on Sunday, December 20, at 3 P.M. Admission free." But just as Sigurlína brought her face right up to the paper to examine the small print, the man closed it so he could look at the back page, and she quickly snapped back to her machine. To this damnable material that didn't want to become a sleeve.

Once the Rubinovs had gone out to the synagogue, Sigurlína fetched some water, put the kettle on the stove, washed up, wiped down her dress and coat, fixed her unbrushed hair, and blew the dust off her hat. Its three red flowers. After that, she set off again, heading that long way for a second time. She walked briskly and with high strides, the sole of her shoe flapping under her boot. A bit like a wind-up soldier.

In front of the museum, a group of people stood waiting to enter. The hall where Brenda was to speak and to promote her book quickly filled. Sigurlína found a seat in the back, tired after her long, trying walk. Instinctively, but discreetly, she sniffed herself—there was clearly no one from her part of town at the event. Two older women were sitting in front of her, but the guests were predominantly men. And it was not only an interest in old Icelandic literature or this new book's subject that had attracted people—so Sigurlína reckoned—but the lecture title as well. An interest in Nordic voyages to the Americas had been growing for some time among American scholars and poets, ever since the Danish antiquarian Carl Christian Rafn published his work *Antiquitates Americanæ* in 1837, but as the century progressed, the matter had taken dramatic shape, a kind of duel between Christopher Columbus and Leifur Eiríksson, a duel culminating in the unveiling of competing monuments to these two protagonists, Leifur in Boston and Columbus in New York. A conflict found a channel in a deep-seated antipathy toward the Catholic heritage of many American immigrants, to their power and influence, especially in New York. Although Brenda had no intention of wading into such political controversies, she certainly was aware of the fact that the debate would arouse interest in her book and draw attention to her own particular emphasis on Guðríður. The plan was to ensure that she, this wife and mother, would enter more boldly into the historical consciousness of the American people.

The ceremony began with a very short and rather confusing presentation by Cesnola himself; he seemed unfamiliar with the topic but offered some pleasant words about the presenter and her invaluable support for the museum. After those words, Brenda herself went to the lectern. A very low chirping resonated around the lecture hall. The sound expressed some kind of reverence: Brenda was a person of stature but equally impressive in appearance and bearing. She was tall, her brown hair loosely tied up. Dark eyes, pale skin. Her face seemingly broad, seemingly soft. She wore a light-colored lace blouse and a dark skirt. A whole bunch of pearls hung around her neck. She was in all actuality a bit like Sigurlína had envisioned her, yet she still gaped in surprise. Maybe it was mostly in reaction to the fact that Brenda existed in reality. In the strange scenario that her life had become these last two months, Sigurlína was not always entirely sure what was real and what wasn't. But now it dawned on her: the recipient of a letter she had fabricated and forged was a person of flesh and blood, and probably wealthy too, and so not completely powerless in this society. Sigurlína had almost gone through with dropping the letter in the mailbox. What if she had changed her mind again? What if she had mailed the letter after all? Maybe fate had swept her feet from under her, causing her to fall to the ground; maybe providence had sent the thief to her to prevent her crime from being carried out?

Brenda Anderson addressed the assembled ladies and gentlemen. Her voice wasn't soft, as her appearance would suggest—it was downright cutting, and when she began to read it became almost sharp. The delivery was brusque as she read from her papers. Brenda told the story of her interest in Nordic voyages, how great an achievement it was in the context of the times, even though it did not leave such a deep mark in the history of Western culture as Columbus' voyage almost five hundred years later. Then she went on to the settlement of Iceland, the Sagas and law-making in the Commonwealth, heroism, the nation's love of freedom, and finally, the remarkable fact that a woman was among the era's explorers. A great woman, unique for her courage and remarkable for her unusual life. Brenda hoped she had managed to paint that picture in her book, offering her interpretation of the

Icelanders' significant historical heritage, a heritage gradually becoming more accessible to English-speaking readers.

Brenda looked up from her papers and addressed her guests once again. Time for the icing on the cake. But she hesitated for a moment. And maybe some of the guests thought she was doing that to build excitement for the next episode in this event. But that was not the case at all; rather, the decision to reveal what was resting on the plinth next to her, behind glass, under a blue velvet cloth, had not been an easy one.

Brenda had been in no doubt about her decision to visit Officer Cooke after receiving the note from him along with Sigurlína's falsified letter, nor had she had any trouble convincing him that she was in a position to track down the owner of the small handbag. But not until she was out of his office and inside her carriage did she dare reach for the object, and right then and there she became convinced that the treasure had fallen into the right hands. Still, Brenda was not a thief; she was of course going to do whatever she could to contact the owner of the belt tip, and she did not expect it to be difficult to offer her money: it was rather clear from the contents of the purse it did not belong to a wealthy woman, her ownership of the treasure probably having come about by some kind of coincidence, as was common for antiquities in far-off lands. Brenda therefore considered herself in an advantageous position toward the owner of the item she coveted. The only problem was that she had few leads that would allow her to find this person. According to Hoffmann's letter, the owner of the object was an Icelander; presumably the woman who had labeled her notebook "Selena Branson."

Over the next few days, Brenda had almost become more interested in the owner of this belt tip than the belt tip itself. She contacted various people she knew who were involved in the housekeeping and settlement of Hoffmann's estate, but no one could say what had happened to the Icelandic girl, not even the estate manager himself, who was at least able to inform Brenda that he had arranged housing for her on Waverly Place, with Mrs. Clark, who was supposed to find her a position in a sewing factory—but that honorable woman had died in a fire a few weeks ago. Only God knew what had happened to the poor girl.

Brenda was in a quandary; she felt more or less as though she was practically stuck with the object. Had even become its protector, after a fashion. And, based on that conviction, she went to meet Cesnola and Marquand, the chair of the board of trustees at the Metropolitan Museum. She told them about the forthcoming publication of her book, emphasized how important its subject matter was for the nation's historical awareness, spoke highly of Hoffmann and his important work in this field, and then laid her cards on the table: this little brass object was from the first half of the eleventh century, had been found buried in Iceland earlier this century, and scholars believed it belonged to her protagonist, the great explorer who had sailed to America with her husband five hundred years before the arrival of Christopher Columbus. The treasure, which was owned by Hoffmann's former assistant, an Icelandic woman named Selena Branson, should therefore rightfully occupy a prominent place in the museum's medieval section, which was being put together. She herself would buy and donate the treasure to the museum; she considered it to be worth fifteen thousand dollars. Of course, that amount was just to convince these gentlemen more fully of the belt tip's value and significance.

Cesnola, who clearly didn't remember Sigurlína bringing the object to his office a few weeks earlier, was somewhat reserved in his reaction to Brenda's words; because of his own ancestry, he was not particularly enthusiastic about ideas that might undermine Columbus' position in American history. And he wasn't entirely convinced about her idea of debuting the treasure with a ceremony and presentation of Guðríður's biography. But he knew that Brenda had plans for further funding for the museum, and he didn't want to jeopardize them. In fact, he suspected, deep down, that his own opinion mattered little; his position within the museum was weak, and he was in debt to the chairman of the board—who, unlike himself, seemed to receive Brenda's idea with much interest. Well, there was a reason for that: Brenda had seeded the soil. A few days before her formal visit to the museum, she had contacted Marquand and made him an offer. She'd offered to sell him a painting she knew he'd longed to acquire ever since her father, Mr. Anderson, had outbid him at an art auction when Brenda was still a teenager. *Portrait of a Man*. Rembrandt.

The meeting in Cesnola's office ended as Brenda's had plotted. Yet she was left to figure out the intricacies of actually purchasing the belt tip, and she had only partially informed these two men of the planned transaction. In desperation, she hired a detective of sorts to hunt down Mrs. Clark's tenants and their fate, but to no avail. In truth, finding a seamstress in this part of the city was a bit like looking for a needle in a haystack.

And thus Brenda was now standing in the museum in front of her audience, suddenly a little unsure of what she'd gotten into, unsure if her defense would hold. So that no one could later accuse her of theft, so that the museum's management might still trust her words, she now described the museum as the owner of the object. However, the statement was made in such a way that no one would truly understand her words except the object's real owner, in the extremely unlikely event she were standing here in the hall; from Brenda's ambiguous phrasing, the audience might either understand that the museum's firm intention was to buy the object, or that it was simply interested in so doing.

An employee of the museum had installed himself in front of the blue veil over the display cabinet. Brenda explained the object, where it had come from, its connection with Guðríður, its value to the museum and to the culture it aimed to share and preserve, and that it would be given pride of place on a pedestal in a new medieval department the museum planned to open soon. Then she gave the employee a signal.

Visitors involuntarily reached out, and some of them stood when Brenda signaled for people to step forward and examine the nearly thousand-year-old belt tip, which had belonged to the first white mother in America. But Sigurlína, in the next-to-last row, went nowhere. She was totally unprepared for what was happening as she hadn't read the lecture advertisement to its end; Rubinov's landlord had closed his newspaper before she could. But shouldn't she have realized that her purse and its contents might end up with Brenda, given that Brenda's name was on the envelope? Or that the thief, disappointed with such slim pickings, might have opened the letter, come to realize the true value of the purse's contents, taken the item to an antique shop, had it assessed, and from there marched it directly to the museum, its authenticity documented in a letter? Assuming the thief was literate, that is.

Sigurlína waited for the shivering sensation to pass. Then she took a deep breath. Should she give herself up? Was she the owner of this precious object? The seller? She got up and walked further into the room, toward the other guests who had gathered around the little glass cabinet. She heard people's silent admiration, saw Brenda appear, her savior, and had suddenly forgotten who the real and rightful owner of the treasure was. She thought she herself was, convinced further when she finally reached the cabinet and was reunited with her old traveling companion, resting there on a shiny, beautiful red surface. She had never found it so beautiful. It lay there, glistening like gold, her little gem, the thing that would put an end to the nightmare in this big city. She moved her face closer to the glass, like she wanted to pass through it, but she was suddenly drawn elsewhere, away from this wonderful dream. On the other side of the glass cabinet stood a young man; unlike her, he had to bend down considerably to regard the object. But now something else has caught his attention. Who is on the other side of these two glass panes? he asks himself. Sigurlína Brandsdóttir, whose father, Brandur Jónsson, was the director of the Antiquarian Collection of Iceland? The man didn't believe his own eyes, and thought he was seeing things. Life's coincidences could hardly be more ridiculous! But Sigurlína believed her eyes, and now that the man's companion had also reached the glass, she was in no doubt. One of his eyes was closed. This was the Englishman she thought had winked at her at the museum in Reykjavík last autumn, as she sat in the knight's throne waiting for her father. At that time the man with the drooping eyelid had been on his way out of the museum with his Icelandic colleague and partner, Dr. Finnsson, a translator of Icelandic sagas, who now shakes his head and reaches out toward the glass cabinet as Sigurlína slowly backs away and disappears into the crowd. She didn't know what to do; she just wandered around to buy time to plan her task to its end. She had to get out of here at once. She headed in the direction of the entrance hall, shooting safely past the guests—but in the end rushing forward and running right into the lecturer and writer herself. Brenda gave out a low yelp; Sigurlína tried to apologize but couldn't say a word, just looked in despair at this commanding, magnificent woman, her beautiful, soft face, then continued along the hallway, out to the lobby, and straight out of the building.

It was dark outside. It was snowing. She ran down the stairs and looked back quickly. Finnsson and the Englishman had exited. They were heading after her. She took to her heels, but when she got out onto the avenue, she didn't know which way to turn. She knew she couldn't run away from them by heading straight south. She longed to head the other way, out into the blue, to where the city ends. She decided to go into the streets to attempt to hide in some side alley or doorway. But there was no such thing; the houses stood in rows and there was nowhere to escape to, unlike downtown. Now she saw them in the distance: they weren't running but instead walking briskly toward her. She continued down the street as fast as she could, but it was no easy feat to run in the snow with the sole of her shoe almost coming off. She was already gasping by the time she came to the next street corner. Then she saw a staircase leading down to a basement in front of the buildings. A hiding place. She flew down the stairs, sat on her haunches, leaned against the wall, and disappeared from view. She could hear her heart racing, she grimaced and whimpered as they approached. Their low conversation, the crunch of the snow under their feet. Then stillness. They'd stopped. Clearly, they'd seen her go down the stairs. But they weren't coming after her. They had no intention of doing so; they were going to force her from her hiding place.

Sigurlína had already experienced despair, hopelessness, and utter abjection on the streets of this city. But this was something completely new. Not only had she come up short, but she had also come to a standstill, unable to move for fear. The shame she felt at this point was the greatest any human being could feel. She looked dead ahead, at a shiny, coal-black door. Next to it, a large bay window. A bustling, ruddy-faced woman was standing by the fireplace and a girl was doing something at a large worktable in the middle of the kitchen. A young, elegantly dressed woman with a baby in her arms had now come down to the kitchen. They were all talking together. Probably about something to do with the Yule celebration. Why couldn't Sigurlína be in there with them? She wouldn't lie about in this house; she would clean all these big pots, boil all this shellfish and open all these oysters. She would fillet the fish, shred the corn, dice the pumpkins, turnips, cabbage, and carrots, peel the potatoes, trim the beans and gooseberries, break the eggs and stir them, melt the butter. Stuff the goose. With all those red apples. The first apple. The first bite. How delicious! Why had her brother accused her of taking a bite of his? And why did her mother look at her so accusingly when Sigurlína denied she was guilty? Her mother had taken both her hands, looked her in the eyes, and said she would believe her if she promised to tell the truth.

The truth? What a brilliant idea! Sigurlína carefully looked up at the stone wall behind her. The besiegers were, after all, a kind of ally of hers: one of them a compatriot and an acquaintance of her father. Now she could finally call for help, unburden herself of everything, and get out of this terrible city. It was as if something broke loose—as if someone had pulled her out of a suit of heavy iron armor. She got up and almost fell down, then walked, with tears in her eyes, hesitantly toward the stairs. Toward the surface of the earth. It was liberating to stand on her feet on the sidewalk, and she felt the lightness and power that came with finally being able to truly return to her former life.

She cleared her throat, stretched herself to her full height, and tried to hold her head high. They turned back to her. She bid them *góða kvöldið*. It was good to hear her mother tongue there in the cold and darkness, feeling herself for the first time in a long time. She moved a little closer. She repeated the greeting, good evening, a little louder than before: "*Góða kvöldið.*" Then they noticed her for the first time. They turned to her, took off their hats as if they were a single man: "Young lady?" Sigurlína took two steps back. Then she looked down and the next moment had dashed across the street. And from there, there was only one direction.

Had she lost her mind—or what? What had she been thinking? That Finnsson and his partner had come all the way to America, in the middle of winter, to a museum to attend a lecture and catch a thief? Sigurlína didn't know if she was relieved by this discovery; she more or less wanted to be plucked off the street. She wanted to be caught as a thief—anything but Rubinov's rabble awaiting her in the foul-smelling darkness and silence. Rubinov. Silent, distant, but always alert. She never knew what to expect at night.

VI

A symposium in Reykjavík, March 1897.
Toward the evening's end.

"I have received a letter from England. It came on the fishing vessel that arrived the day before yesterday." The Governor leans back a little in his seat as if to indicate that he will not get up any time soon, now that he has finally reached the heart of the matter, the actual purpose of tonight's meeting. He refreshes his guests' memory on Dr. Finnsson, and the company responds by nodding slowly and surely; with that gesture the men express their respect for the correspondent. They will prick up their ears.

The Governor says Finnsson was in New York City at the end of last year along with an English colleague, Dr. Cook, on their way from Chicago. And there in the big city, the two men attended a lecture on a subject that had caught their attention: a new biography of Guðríður Þorbjarnardóttir, by the aforementioned Brenda Anderson. At the end of this talk, which the men found rather trifling—although it was admirably inspired by the ideal of Nordic voyages to America in the face of Columbus' legacy—the program took a rather unexpected turn. An announcement was being made, an object being unveiled, an object the museum intended to buy, a treasure believed to have belonged to Guðríður: a belt tip made of brass on which the guests were invited to set eyes. Finnsson mentioned that at first glance the object had hardly appeared to be anything more than a small part of a belt tip; on closer inspection, however, he thought it looked more like a brooch. But what had urgently prompted the pair, Finnsson and Cook, to request a meeting with the director of the museum—one Cesnola—was the alleged origin of the artifact. They were ushered into his office right away, but Finnsson immediately got the feeling that the curator knew little about the item, even though he was able to inform them that it was a gift to the museum from Brenda herself, who had bought it for fifteen thousand dollars from a woman of Icelandic descent, someone related to Franz Hoffmann—he didn't remember the name. And that was that: Cesnola had no more to say on the matter, and it was clear from his approach that he had neither the interest nor the time for this unexpected meeting. When the comrades had modestly expressed their doubts about the object's origins and were on their way out, the curator had, however, called after them that the woman's name was Branson. He seemed to have suddenly remembered. Selena? He wasn't sure.

Selena Branson? This information had not directly allayed Finnsson's suspicions that there might be a trick in the game, a total falsification of history, but after he returned to England he had another epiphany: another Icelandic treasure surfaced in his mind—a tongue-shaped brooch he had seen at the Antiquarian Collection in Reykjavík the previous autumn. The purport of his letter to the Governor was therefore primarily a request for an investigation into the theft.

"A young woman of Icelandic descent. Selena Branson." The Governor rises from his seat. He goes out to the living room window and watches the snowflakes hang in the air, the light from the white earth illuminating the black darkness. "And now I ask you, dear comrades," he says, "whether Sigurlína Brandsdóttir, the daughter of scholar and scribe Brandur Jónsson from Kot in Skagafjörður, doesn't enter into things at this juncture?"

After the men variously expressed their displeasure at this deed, or their doubt that there might be any connection between little Lína and Hoffmann, they discussed the nature of the crime and the possible punishment; they cogitated on the amount of money; they voiced uncertainty that such a small thing could be worth so much—until Jón, the Editor, politely jumped from his thoughts and bid them "Stop this nonsense!" They have nothing to go on yet. The right thing to do would be to contact Brandur himself before deciding anything in this matter. The assembly looks at the young man in amazement, then at each other, and nods: Of course, the first step is to go to see Brandur. And that sound decision, of course, must be toasted. But the liqueur glasses are empty! The carafe is not on the table. Where is the girl? She went out to refill the bottle. A long time ago.

A small flower, coal-black.

The cabinet stands against a wall, almost in a corner, where few people pay attention to it—except for the visitor who comes to the museum every Sunday just to see the object it houses. And, after so doing, attempts to talk to the curator, introducing herself as the owner of this antiquity, hoping to recover it. The longer it lies behind this glass, the more likely it is that its preservation will be questioned and thus her crime discovered. Sigurlína had, it's true, originally gone to see the museum director hoping to achieve this very outcome, but at the time she'd been compelled by events and out of her wits. She had had no other choice if she wanted to escape Rubinov's clutches and return to Iceland.

But now it's the brooch that holds her captive; she is on her way home to Iceland, but cannot leave without it. After Brenda's lecture, after she had addressed the strangers standing in the street—the ones she had thought to reconcile with, believing they were Finnsson and his English companion—she had stayed in her lair with her mind so utterly unruly that she didn't sleep a wink all night. The next morning she was more or less delirious sewing sleeves, only recovering her senses whenever she was disturbed by the thought of the object behind the glass, reminding herself how it had ended up there, wondering how long it would lie there before she was hunted down as a thief, asking herself whether she was indeed a thief, who was a thief, she herself, Sigurlína, maybe Selena, or her father, or Mr. Watson, or the pickpocket—the villainous Mary O'Reilly, whom she never saw and whose identity she didn't know—or Brenda Anderson, the Metropolitan Museum, the director of which she must talk to as soon as possible—although of course that was fraught with problems, because all this nonsense Brenda and the museum had indulged in was due to an act Sigurlína had certainly committed, though the correspondence was not a crime in itself because she had never intended to mail the letter and never did so, was it a crime to forge a letter that was not intended to be delivered to the recipient, and if it was a crime, against whom was it committed, Hoffmann, the Icelanders, the history of Iceland, perhaps Guðríður herself, she was not sure, but when she began to imagine the punishment that awaited her if it came to light, Sigurlína began to tremble and to breathe hard and deep, feeling as if someone was pulling on her skirt, that she was being sucked down into the dirty floor of the sickening sweatshop, with nothing to hold on to but a sewing needle from the little cushion on the table in front of her and a black tuft of twine lying in the rubbish next to it, a thread she managed to force through the eye of the needle and then through the coarse coat material, up and down with such zeal until the stamen formed, the crown of eight petals, the base, the stem, leaves, and her hands were bloody, her body exhausted after this vigorous, meticulus work, and she did not remember how that day ended or how the next one started, how Christmas passed, only recalled waking up on the second day of the new year, Rubinov jostling her awake on his way out of the house and up Rivington Street, up to Barbieri's factory, where he put his heavy load on the table by the buttonholer who lazily got up from his morning coffee to start his specialized work— but it was not until Rubinov was back out on the street that this tall, energetic man, the buttonholer, paused to observe a strange anomaly in the production on one sleeve, asking himself how it came to be, then calling the pleater, who shrugged and called the hemmer, who called the presser, who took the sleeve, examined the material and then looked at his comrades, saying that this needed the witness of Mr. Barbieri, who now appeared as if he had sensed this quiet uproar among his men, and when the Italian tailor had scrutinized these stiches, this little coal-black flower on the sleeve, *Dryas octopetala* on a dark gray surface, sewn into the coarse fabric with the most delicate threads and with such great art that it was hard to believe that th work had been done by a human hand, he began to nod, he grabbed the coat from the table and walked out of his workshop.

The afternoon of the same day, after a bit of an argument with her Russian master, Sigurlína had become one of five seamstresses for Mrs. Barbieri, a dressmaker at 5th Avenue and 27th Street. The tailor's sister. And he, this well-dressed and friendly man, had accompanied Sigurlína there himself, to his sister's home, declaring that her big brother had solved her problems for the time being. But all this was ill-thought-through: the man had half-promised Sigurlína lodging, without knowing anything about his sister's current circumstances, and she seemed alarmed to see this new employee. Not that Sigurlína bore traces of her former squalor, but her sole belongings were in one white cloth bag. Yet the brother promised first-class craftsmanship and so Sigurlína got a small attic room in the dressmaker's home.

After all, it made sense, for the working hours in this house were long, with work sometimes continuing until after midnight. Mostly in silence, no one directly asking about her identity, the topics they discussed limited to the complex tasks they had to solve. But everything was better than the monotonous drudgery in the cold, shit, and damp of Rubinov's little sweatshop. Easier to escape the thought of her possible fate inside a warmer, cleaner studio, better off sewing flowers into silk, attaching pearls to velvet and buttons made of precious stones, setting lace on collars. And though Sigurlína didn't ask any questions, she soon began to suspect that something big was going on, the cause of the strange silence. These were no ordinary clothes. These were costumes, and when the papers began to publish news of the biggest and most glorious dance in history, the girls themselves, the artisans, knew they were involved in creating an adventure.

Nearly twelve hundred guests from New York and other nearby cities were rumored to have been invited to the event, which evidently was no old-fashioned masked ball, a wild joy of mysterious guests floating around with glittering masks over their faces. No, this was clearly intended to be a more formal gathering, was in fact a highly ambitious attempt to recreate the bygone eras of history: according to the invitation, guests were to dress up in the costumes of royalty and nobles from early modern Europe. Thus the possibilities were not exactly inexhaustible, leading to much effort seemingly spent on historical accuracy rather than originality and glory. In other words, it wasn't enough to adorn oneself with precious stones and silk; the immoderately rich now set their sights on being able to embellish real historical valuables in the form of clothes and jewelry. But the game was made yet more difficult for the guests because the hosts, Cornelia Bradley Martin and her husband, had sent their invitations on unusually short notice. And they had done so on purpose: by preventing visitors from ordering their costumes from Paris, as was customary for such entertainments, the happening would stimulate the nation's domestic economy, which wasn't back on its feet after the financial collapse of 1893. The scheme—which had been criticized by priests and other influential society moralists as a corrupt play, a contest over greatness, in difficult times—certainly benefitted Sigurlína's circumstances and finances, as she now earned three times as much as she had with Rubinov. She finally foresaw returning home in the spring.

But of course, one little piece of finery behind glass put a dent in the bill. When Sigurlína had been sitting and sewing from morning to evening for over a month, the projects gradually lessened; the day of the dance, February 10, was approaching. The last costume, a hell of a silk dress for one Madame de Pompadour, left Barbieri on Saturday night, February 6. That evening Sigurlína went to sleep in her little closet, unsure of what tomorrow would bring, other than one more visit to the art museum. One more attempt to talk to the director.

Those were anxious journeys. What were the chances that the deed would surface, the forgery of the letter from Hoffmann to Brenda, the falsification of the story itself, when she presented herself as the owner of the brooch? As time went on, however, it dawned on her that such a suspicion would probably have to be based on some knowledge of the treasure itself. Therefore, the suspicion of forgery would not arise until the origin of the object and its history had been disputed. And it was highly unlikely that someone within the museum had such insight. Sigurlína would probably never have to deny the crime outright to the museum's officials or to Brenda herself in the near future. It was first and foremost a matter of getting the treasure from the museum as soon as possible, before its preservation was questioned by experts on the subject. Before speculation reached the shores of Iceland. She was left with no other option than to convince Cesnola that she was the rightful owner of the object. And if the brooch had fallen into Brenda's hands as part of the contents of her little purse, she would have no problem proving it was hers. These were her thoughts as she walked along the frozen ground toward the museum. Purseless. Of course.

But everything went the same way as before. Her request was rejected. The curator was not available. Could she wait? The employee's response to her question was non-existent, but Sigurlína decided to stick around and think things through. She could hardly leave the building with nothing in her hands after yet another trip. She settled down on the bench in the small side room, looked intently in front of herself, and thought of the next steps. Steps she would take in the direction of the small display case, as usual. She looked through the glass. It was as if this object were her grounding; the fact that it was lying there behind the glass proved that the events of the last few weeks were not a solitary hallucination.

But locked inside the cabinet, it was also a threat, something that would sooner or later explode and cause her terror. Do away with her honor.

Sigurlína stroked the glass, pressed it, felt the door budge. Poked her little finger into the keyhole. She cursed very low and looked around. She clenched her fist and kept her eyes closed. But when she opened them again, she involuntarily released the tension, bent down slightly and pushed her face up against the glass. What the hell! She got up, took two steps back, and stood in front of the case, and then was all at once rushing from the hall. In desperation, she hurried from room to room, shouting in her head for the guard. But on what business? Was she going to report a robbery? Was it not more likely that the museum had refrained from displaying this object with scant connection to the history it aimed to preserve? And didn't the fact that the object was no longer on display mean that she was safe and sound? She looked ahead, at her reflection in a large display cabinet, the look of horror that moved over her face when she saw what was visible behind the glass: a Cypriot limestone cat sticking out its tongue! What if the item had been removed on suspicion that its origin was not what the museum had claimed? Wouldn't she be in a worse position than ever? Shouldn't she hold off on raising the alarm?

She hobbled along the icy sidewalk on her way back, taking pains; her mind could no longer cope with the ridiculous situation in which it had once again found itself. At Barbieri's, the maid greeted her with the message that the lady wanted to see her right away in the sewing room. Sigurlína took off her hat, knocked and pushed open the door. The midday sun illuminated the large studio, the rays fell on a sapphire blue surface, the material covering the large cutting board. The cutter, an older woman, was laying pieces of brown paper on the fabric under the watchful eye of the dressmaker. She nodded eagerly but threw up her hands in despair when she saw Sigurlína. Barbieri was a fast talker. She looked straight into her eyes, spoke in fast phrases and gestured with both hands. They weren't finished yet. They had one more big task ahead of them. As soon as the skirt was tailored—the Italian master pointed out the sunbaked wool that was now being cut—Sigurlína would have to start sewing. Embroidering. She handed her an image of a small flower with freely drawn lines; she then let her hand crawl along the length of the material. Four meters, she said, and held out as many fingers. She then held out three fingers: the days until her deadline.

There were no precise instructions as to where exactly the flowers should be placed on the skirt, or how they should be embroidered. Flower stitchwork? Probably. The material was wool, heavy, yet so delicate that it shone under the light from the lamp next to her chair. And the texture was wonderfully soft; Sigurlína felt like she was petting a small calf when she slid her hand along the material while studying the drawing. Eight petals, a stem and three leaves with golden wool thread. Nothing else really, so she had to design it herself somehow to fit on the material along the hemline.

On Tuesday evening, Sigurlína had finished sewing three meters, and had about ten flowers left. That night she worked until morning, when the skirt was sewn on the upper part of the dress and hemmed. A simple but elegant dress for a medieval princess ready to be delivered by Barbieri, who this time wanted Sigurlína by her side.

The carriage parked outside a magnificent but not very large house on Fifth Avenue. An elderly steward stood in the doorway and greeted the women carrying the costume into the house. The approach reminded Sigurlína of Hoffmann's home: a large and elegant lobby with a stone staircase up to the second story, where the two of them followed the steward as though they were one person. Upstairs, a girl appeared, almost as if out of the wall, and opened a double door into a large, dark room. From there came a heavy, exotic smell, but sweet and good; everywhere was full of furniture, large and dark, a carved canopy bed, hand-painted screens. The lady of the house welcomed the newcomers, hugged Barbieri, while two girls took care to lay the woolen dress on a deep red, upholstered Ottoman in the middle of the room. The owner of the dress expressed her admiration by putting both her hands to her mouth and nose then throwing off her silk robe to try on the costume with the help of the older maid, who stroked the wool once the woman was dressed, as if to verify and underline how well the garment fit her body. Then she held out the hem. The woman admired the golden flowers. It's perfect, she said, but Barbieri pointed with a smile at Sigurlína, who stood like a ghost in the middle of the room. They looked into each other's eyes.

And what? Perhaps Sigurlína was too tired to recognize a woman she had only seen on one occasion, and from a distance, in strange and unexpected circumstances? At least she was too weak to put two and two together: Brenda and a costume of a medieval princess. Her head really couldn't fit much more than the simple conclusion that they probably all looked the same, these beautiful upper-class roses floating about the city streets. Moreover, it was a completely different voice than the one that had sounded so memorable inside the museum's room on December 20. That voice had been sharp and high-pitched, but the voice that now quietly gave one of the girls the command to "fetch it" was gentle and almost seductive. But it was obeyed at once: the younger maid came along with a black pillow in her hands; she held it in front of her like a tray. On the pillow was a leather strap that both girls began to tie around the woman's narrow waist. It was a kind of loop knot, so one end of the girdle lay down the skirt and the woman swung it side to side on her way to a large mirror in one corner of the room. The girls retreated. But the ghost, Sigurlína, awakened. She walked slowly toward the blue-clad princess who addressed her own reflection with a sweeping, victorious smile. It was as if the princess Brenda had been pulled into another world because she didn't notice Sigurlína enter the frame, standing there as if in a trance, with her eyes fixed upon a small brass piece attached to the end of the leather belt.

Gudrid

Brenda Anderson had initially resolved to turn down the invitation to the Bradley Martin ball. Over the years she had developed a contempt for such gatherings of the aristocracy, where everything was up for sale for the sake of individual glory. Ava Vanderbilt's historic costume ball of 1883 had set the tone for such events: a woman wearing a stuffed cat on her head, another wearing a dress lit up with electric lights. But this invitation constrained the imagination somewhat, and the nature of the direct instructions in the invitation aroused Brenda's disdain: the prank was downright ridiculous. Although it was purportedly for fun, the ball was nothing more than a pathetic attempt by the upper class to hide its lack of sophistication and tradition, its way to acquire what it most craved and what money could not buy: blue blood. What's more, it would call for overwhelming adornment and distasteful hypocrisy at a time when social inequality was ever growing.

But just when Brenda was in the midst of her moralizing, she had an idea. Instead of hating these ahistorical souls and their antics, she would protest their fetish by attending while ignoring their instructions—taking a stand, in a plain costume from the past, of a nation few people had heeded. She would go as the Icelandic explorer Guðríður Þorbjarnadóttir! Of course, the idea was partly a way to promote her own interests; indeed Brenda was rather more extreme in her historical vanity than her fellow citizens, none of whom had a treasure in their possession, taken off display from the Metropolitan Museum in order to accent their costume and the figure it represented. What's more, her last-minute ingenuity had caused poor Sigurlína, one of the downtrodden in the big city with whom Brenda purported to sympathize, to almost sew her hands together making Brenda's vision come true.

The dance took place at the Waldorf Hotel, on the corner of 5th Avenue and 33rd Street. It was freezing cold; the streets were icy. A large number of civilians had gathered outside the building, but a guard fence of three hundred policemen kept them at a reasonable distance from the entrance, where servants wearing perukes and dressed in golden uniforms lay a bright red carpet along the sidewalk. Soon the street was filled with horse-drawn carriages, with their attendant noise, but instead of booing the rich, as had been expected, the people began to welcome the ornate and glorious guests: royalty and princes of the past. There were about eight copies of Henry the Eighth, ten Madames de Pompadour, seven Madames de Maintenon, three Catherine the Greats, fifty Marie Antoinettes, one hundred acting as Louis the Fourteenth. There were Napoleons and Josephines, Joans of Arc, English judges, French courtiers and Revolutionary leaders, Dutch officials as depicted by Rembrandt, the Infanta Margarita from Velázquez's painting, George Washingtons, Counts of Monte Cristo, Queen Isabella of Spain. No Columbus?

"Amateurs and boors," thought Brenda, as the hosts, Louis XV and Mary Stuart, Queen of Scots, with Mary Antoinette's diamond bracelet around her neck, led the elite of New York City along the gleaming floor of the Hall of Mirrors in some kind of fifteenth-century courtly dance—set to Beethoven's music, no less! And with that performance, a three-hour dance program began, in which Brenda took full part, driven by the attention that her plain elegance attracted among the guests, many of whom were so armored that they had difficulty moving. However, no one really discerned what her costume was supposed to represent: some understandably thought she was a medieval princess, and few knew of her new book about Guðríður. Brenda, on the other hand, didn't tire of educating her countless dance partners about her protagonist, to variously lukewarm reactions, although most guests were quite interested in the belt around her middle, particularly its age.

But then came the setback. At midnight, as the dinner itself was about to begin, Brenda realized that she was not the only mutineer on board this sinking ship. Richard Welling, lawyer and social reformer, had radically deviated from the recommendations of the hosts, garnering the attention and admiration of many guests by dressing as a Native American chief, his costume fitted according to learned men's advice. His accomplice was Pocahontas herself, Miss Anne Morgan, the daughter of the absent J. P. Morgan, who attracted no less attention for her originality. This was an explicit and powerful statement that everyone understood, a past that truly challenged the idea behind the greatest ball of all time. A simple woolen garment and an Icelandic antiquity of brass had very little significance in comparison. A bit of an interloper at that historic showdown.

So small, with such a large, tattered hat.

Brenda didn't remember when she had left the hotel, but after a twenty-eight-course formal dinner that began at midnight, she was fatigued. Her carriage, however, was nowhere to be seen, and so she'd gotten ensnared into taking a ride with an old family friend, a drunken Henry the Eight in full armor. The journey home was not long, but when the carriage stopped in front of her house, it became clear that the King of England, the ladies' man he was, had an unrealistic idea of how the evening would end. The ensuing fight was particularly embarrassing, and fierce enough that Brenda had to half-break out of the carriage. It was, however, more in a state of annoyance than actual disorder that she waved her steward away at the doorway and elbowed her way into the living room. She threw herself on the sofa and cursed herself to sleep.

She had only slept for little more an hour when someone opened the door, then closed it again, waking her. She lay in the darkness, her head full of last night's scenes, her heart strangely empty. She got up with careful movements but as she was about to rise from the couch, she was suddenly reminded of how the armored blockhead had tugged at her belt to reel her in as she sat next to him in the carriage. The moment resurfaced, for now she saw how much his clumsy actions had cost her. The belt tip!

Brenda was at once on all fours, furiously crawling around on the floor, under the sofa and table. She went into the corridor and ordered her steward to go out and look for the object. But it was dark and everything was submerged in snow and the wind was gusting, so the poor man didn't have an easy time of it, dressed up as he was, not to mention half blind. Two of her girls had come in and been sent out to shovel the snow and move it about with their bare hands. But nothing could be found. Maybe the tip had fallen off the leather strap inside the carriage. The search should at least wait until dawn. Brenda called her people in and went to get some rest herself.

She was still fast asleep at the time Sigurlína was rising from a sleepless night. Going with Barbieri to visit Brenda and seeing the belt around her waist had once again changed Sigurlína's position and plans. Now she knew why the artifact had disappeared from the museum; now she had another chance to recover it. And she had to do it as soon as possible because when they had returned, she and the dressmaker, the latter made it clear to her that in all likelihood she could no longer keep her on: the Bradley Martin masked ball had been a one-off project; the demand for custom sewing was on the decline and hand-sewing—such work was now done increasingly via machine. Then Barbieri had handed over her wages and Sigurlína reckoned it was enough for a fare back home.

Damnable, evil object! It was as if someone up above was constantly moving it about, making it disappear and reappear in order to test her. But after her sleepless night, Sigurlína was certain: She had to get it back, to try to talk to Brenda now that she knew where she lived.

It wasn't very easy to make it through the streets this Wednesday morning as they still hadn't been shoveled. But Sigurlína pressed on: "My name is Selena, I'm from Iceland, I have come to inquire about an item I lost and I suspect you have found, I need to obtain it immediately because I am to sail home to Iceland soon, yes, I too am so glad we're finally meeting, yes, Hoffmann, such a sad story, the poor man, no, of course one cannot be certain but the treasure was found during an excavation near the farm where Guðríður lived in her last years, it's a guess but yes, I was given it a long time ago, no, not that, something else, I only recently acquired it and have never been separated from it but I have decided to transfer it to our museum in Reykjavík so this poor nation of mine can show foreigners that significant objects and artifacts exist in our country as much as in other nations, a hundred dollars, that's a generous offer but I cannot sell the piece, you see, it truly belongs to the Icelandic nation. Iceland needs it."

When Sigurlína reached her destination and Brenda's small palace appeared out of the snowdrifts, she paused on the sidewalk and questioned herself for the last time, cleansing herself of any suspicion of having forged a letter and a story. Then she knocked on the door, completely unaware of the customs and traditions that were upheld by visiting women in this part of the city. Indeed, the steward answered in the negative, Brenda was otherwise engaged, it was not yet twelve o'clock. But Sigurlína had no intention of letting things go this time and she talked on and on until the steward closed the door, asking her to wait.

Brenda had woken up by then. She was sitting up in bed, reading the day's papers, a daily column expressing placid displeasure at last night's event, discussing at length the two Native American costumes and the deserved attention they aroused. And she herself was mentioned, the darling of the gossipmongers, the wealthy spinster who had come to the dance alone, without a companion, dressed as Guðríður, an Icelandic explorer, the mother of the first white child in America. Brenda's heart pounded as she read on. Unlike other guests who had dressed in silk and adorned themselves with historic gemstones, Brenda wore an unostentatious woolen dress, but she had also worn a remarkable object: a thousand-year-old belt tip, formerly owned by Guðríður. These were more or less Brenda's words at the event, and as much as she had longed to stand out that night and draw attention to her protagonist, she wasn't sure if she wanted it all set down in print for publication. Especially now that she might have lost the object! Brenda threw away the paper and was about to summon her people, to get them to contact Henry the Eighth's residence and to continue searching outside in the snow, when the girl entered and informed her that an Icelandic woman was standing at the front door and insisting on talking with her. An Icelandic woman? Brenda asked her girl to leave the room briefly. For a moment, she looked straight ahead. Was it the owner of the bag with the embroidered little flower? Hoffmann's assistant? Selena Branson? The woman she had hunted high and low for, trying to find her? Come to retrieve her treasure?

Brenda went over to the large front-facing windows, put both hands on the thick curtains, stuck her face through the slit and gently leaned against the white gauzy material. Snow. Sunshine. Selena. So small, with such a large, tattered hat, shuffling about on the doorstep that the men had now finished shoveling. Badly dressed. Without a purse. Without anything. And then Brenda would extend her warm welcome: "I am glad to have you in my house, to finally meet an Icelander, to finally have an opportunity to sort out this complication, to discuss this little object I received from the police station, of course my name and address were the only thing they had to go on, but when I couldn't find you myself, it occurred to me to draw attention to the matter in connection with a lecture I gave at the art museum, a lecture on my book about Guðríður, the owner of the belt tip, according to the hypothesis, is that not the case? Of course, I want to know all about the history behind the artifact and to complete the purchase, a thousand dollars, so I can donate it to the museum, a museum that will soon be one of the largest and most famous museums in the world, where the history of your nation will be well preserved. Receive its deserved place alongside classical culture."

The girl fastened the button at her mistress's nape while Brenda loosely put her hair up. She went downstairs and gave her steward a signal to direct the Icelandic guest in. She didn't go to the living room as usual, but stood in the lobby ready to welcome Sigurlína. But when the door opened, no one was on the doorstep. Sigurlína had gone back out onto the path and walked slowly and hesitantly toward the street. Then she looked back over her shoulder. Her face was ghostly, her eyes desperate, but it was hard to tell if the girl was more scared or angry, so suddenly did she start running along the street. At pace, heading east.

The steward shrugged, closed the door, and looked in amazement at his mistress, who had been going to call out to her guest but had not uttered a word, just rolled her shoulders and pretended nothing was afoot. Alone in the living room, however, she felt her heart rate increase as Sigurlína's face nestled more firmly in her head. It all reanimated last night's aftereffects, the shame the day's newspaper had sought to convey in words of polite judgment. Brenda was one of the group, no matter how she struggled to convince herself otherwise: constantly searching for validation, her wealth as her weapon. Appearing rather than existing. A cowardly fool dreaming of challenging tradition but, in her vanity, losing valuables that didn't belong to her, the sole possession of a tiny Icelandic woman, a woman of flesh and blood with a cheap, worn-out hat on her head. A woman who had come to her house as an emissary of that very truth. That was the only explanation Brenda could find for the strange incident she had just witnessed. She closed her eyes, leaned back in her desk chair and sat down on the pillow with her legs apart, wearing pale pink silk shoes with a lace flower on the instep.

Had Henry the Eighth's driver been contacted? Shouldn't she send her people to search the snow in front of her house? Brenda rose from her chair and reached for the small purse that lay on the bureau. She squeezed the bag. Eight cream-white petals, a pistil and a light-yellow stigma. A very short stem ending in three green leaves. A hardy, easy-to-please plant that could withstand windy, cold climates.

A Recompense

Sigurlína was about three meters behind the wooden cart
the horse was pulling ever onward. She had no idea where
the cart was headed, she was tiring fast, and she thought it
impossible she could speed up enough to reach into the back
of it. Too out of breath to call out to the plowman to ask
him to stop, anxious not to take her eyes off the hollow at
the top of the pile of snow that had formed when the man
swung his shovel for the last time to complete his work in
front of Brenda's house. It was a powerful swing—the snow
had to make it all the way from the shovel to the top of the
tall heap—and accompanied by the man's groan, it caused
Sigurlína to turn to the street in time to see something flung
into the air. It was an incredible sight, like some kind of illu-
sion, but she immediately headed out onto the sidewalk. Just
then the door to Brenda's house opened. Sigurlína glanced
back for a moment, at Brenda and her steward in the doorway, terrified that she would now lose sight of what was floating above the cart, even though she knew it could hardly be
what she thought it was. The object landed on the snowdrift;

it dropped down inside the snow, leaving a hole Sigurlína could still make out as she goes after the cart, feeling sure she was chasing something that was nothing, that her destiny was nothing but running hopelessly after the cart, running anywhere at all, always on the run, chasing vague dreams of nothing, trying to make something of hersellf, taking the floor for the sake of making herself heard:

They had all been settled into the living room in Aðalstræti last spring, a group of Jón's friends, discussing everything between heaven and earth, and Sigurlína couldn't help but listen as she sat and sewed with the little girl. Mostly it was progressive drivel. There was talk of Icelandic education, and as Sigurlína walked past the living room on her way out, Jón suddenly interrupted one of his friends: "What's going to happen to Icelandic nationality, then?" And before any of the group could answer this vast question, Sigurlína turned around: "It will finally come to an end."

At first there was silence, then young men started laughing, by which time she had her coat on. She walked along the street, cursing herself for her outspokenness, her nonsense, when she realized someone was following her. She had no intention of answering for her silly behavior so she sped up her walk and turned into an alley. But that didn't help; she was grabbed by the shoulder. Forced to turn around. His gaze was tired but somehow focused and serious; his wide face had high cheekbones; his dark hair was combed back. She had left her purse behind. They looked into each other's eyes for a moment until she could no longer hold back; she began to giggle. He smiled, at first a little forced, but then he began to giggle, too, with his hair falling right into his face. And there they stood facing each other, bursting out laughing, until he suddenly fell silent, becoming serious again but not distant, as he sometimes was, but close. Closer to her than ever. At that point, she understood how a moment could last forever, because she was still in the alley even when she was back home. She threw herself into bed, wanting only to lie there and remain in her dreams, though downstairs there were flowers waiting to be sewn onto a skirt and ribbons, ancient stories to be written down one more time. And she rose, of course, she sat at her seat, she worked until nightfall. A servant and slave to Icelandic culture.

She cannot go any further. She stops, watches the cart pull away. She walks slowly in its wake, thinking of turning back to where she had left off outside Brenda's home, then suddenly starts walking faster when she realizes what's happening. The snow is going to be dumped into the East River! Maybe that will solve all her problems? No, probably not—so she continues at a pace, moving now with tremendous power, with the fate of an entire nation resting on her pluck. She sees where the plowman opens the cart's tailgate, but when he tips it, she realizes the river is frozen under the snowdrifts the men have been competing to dump into the river. By the time she's reached the riverbank, the man has emptied the cart; Sigurlína walks straight out onto the ice. It will take some time to root in the pile, which of course has gotten mixed up with the rest of the snow, but the work is worth doing. She scrapes and rummages like mad, her small hands ice-cold, but she finds nothing, and rushes hither and thither, getting further out on the ice sheet. She hears shouting and hollering, then again, louder, as she stumbles. She's about to get to her feet but falls back. The ice is breaking up and she's on all fours on the unstable floe and doesn't dare move. Two men standing on the bank of the river are about to leave shore, come to her, but as soon as one of them jumps out onto the ice, her own raft shifts. Sigurlína slips straight into the freezing water.

She emits a loud, strange sound that stifles her intense heartbeats. She takes a few floundering strokes in the water but soon disappears below the surface and is swept under the ice. She kicks with her feet but makes no headway. She continues to swallow the water. Suddenly, heat flows through her body, and gradually she sees light penetrating the water. She tries to make it there but feels herself sinking deeper. She stares at the light, at something that has fallen into the water and seems to be heading toward her. She tries to move her legs but they feel paralyzed. As the object approaches, and she recognizes it for what it is, she regains her strength. Slowly, she raises one hand to try to seize what she came here to demand. But—what else could happen?—the treasure slips away from her, over and over again. Just when she is finally about to grab it, she is pulled up by a powerful force. Everything becomes nothing.

VII

Reykjavík. At the beginning of the summer of 1897.

He had gotten an idea for a little poem and was about to set it down when he received the Governor's summons. Right now? The breathless messenger didn't know, so he dared not do anything but leave at once. Jón, the Editor. Always with the blonde girl's face in his head, with second thoughts persisting as to what happened this winter, a lunatic declaration, a damnable confusion that wound around him, an idea that had mostly come from others, and which he hadn't thought of as such a bad thing to begin with. But he hadn't understood what he was signing up for, and he had finally ended the engagement when it came to light that the young Danish widow, the tall and attractive Bodil, who had been sent to Iceland through family friends to convalesce after her husband's death, had no desire to settle in Reykjavík. Must he then leave the country, leave the newspaper and the work he had so long pursued? He was in a quandary and buried himself in work, always full of opinions even though he was ever careful in his affairs, avoided contentiousness, took a moderate stance on the constitution. For he was political in a different way, a campaigner for an Icelandic university; he wanted to raise proper edifices for the museums in Iceland so their cultural heritage wouldn't have to be tucked away here and there in dusty trunks. That, he believed, was what made him a progressive, although he feared the influence of foreigners, especially those wealthy entrepreneurs. Still, he wondered deep down how Iceland would ever rise from the abyss and explode onto the scene as an independent state in this new century without the aid of foreign capital.

Money. Now he turned onto Austurstræti and it appeared before him, this great building that was under construction. In the damp Reykjavík air, giant stones hung on wires on their way up to the walls. Down on the ground, workers were clearing rocks, while up on the roof, at the top of the scaffolding, stood men in suits; at the front, almost right by the edge, was one of Iceland's most powerful officials, the bank director himself, the animal lover who was also a shipowner, a merchant, a town delegate, and a member of parliament. On the boards of many organizations. Just what Icelandic authorities approved of as a sign of great diligence.

Jón reckoned the building was far too large for Iceland's only working bank, open just a few days each week, with but one million króna in savings. But this construction in the very center of town was meant to last, and no doubt part of this splendid structure could be used for other purposes. Maybe as a museum—like always, upstairs. Upstairs in churches, upstairs in parliament, upstairs in the bank. Jón disliked the idea. Cultural heritage shouldn't be stored in a bank.

The Governor welcomed the young member of him group, who believed he wanted to talk to him about the banking issue and the voices criticizing Iceland's financial management. But that's not at all the leader's concern, this conservative windbag who is constantly criticized for being indifferent to the nation's future; instead, the Governor wanted to turn to the meeting that took place in this very room late last the winter, to the letter from Dr. Finnsson and to the treasure in the Metropolitan Museum, to the symposium about Sigurlína that had ended with the decision that Jón, as a board member of the Icelandic Antiquarian Collection, should meet with Brandur and ask him about his daughter's travels and the alleged theft from the Collection. From that conversation, he had seemingly received little in the way of information, and the matter was forgotten. But now the Governor has suddenly become interested again. He wanted to know exactly what transpired between them.

Jón told him how Brandur had been lying on his death bed, unaware that anything had disappeared from the museum. All he knew about his daughter's travels was a message she had left. Here, of course, the old man hadn't told Jón the whole truth, because the Governors' maid—Brandur's niece—had rushed like wildfire through snowdrifts in the pitch darkness of Reykjavík that winter night, shaking off two crazy horses and one wild water bearer to tell Brandur everything that happened during the symposium. Exactly the way she'd heard it through the door panel. Brandur knew what Jón knew, but Jón didn't know what Brandur knew— even though the dying man's sardonic expression momentarily aroused his suspicion. And the Governor didn't know what Jón knew when he said he didn't remember exactly what was written on the note Brandur had given him, other than that Sigurlína had gone to Scotland and would return in the spring. But Jón actually remembered the note word for word, the note Sigurlína had left on her father's desk before she ran with her trunk down to Geirsbryggja the year before; he'd taken it without Brandur seeing. And he'd read it many, many times since: *Do not be angry with me, my father. I have answered one of your letters without permission. I have taken from your desk a little letter from Hoffmann in New York, and thus complied with his request for a scribe for a winter. I'm doing it for you. Although I hardly know why.*

Thus, Jón was pretty convinced that Sigurlína was Selena, the woman connected to Hoffmann and Brenda, who had sold an Icelandic belt tip to the museum in New York. That artifact could hardly have come from anywhere other than Reykjavík's Antiquarian Collection. Reporting the crime would be simple, but he had no intention of being part of that investigation. So he explained that he had no further information on the matter for the Governor, who now leaned forward to get something out of his bottom desk drawer. He set the item on the table and asked Jón to look at it. A brown parcel mailed from New York. Marked Selena Branson. The Governor said that the package had been lying in the post office for several weeks and that the Postmaster had contacted him after eventually deciding to see what was inside. The Governor reached for the package contents and handed them to Jón.

It was a woman's bag—a purse of black velvet with flowers sewn on it. Holtasóley; *Dryas octopetala*. Jón knew this bag well, and he involuntarily brought it for a moment to his nose. But it smelled different than he remembered. He had taken it off the console table in the front hall of his house on Aðalstræti last spring on his way after Sigurlína, who had run from the house after saying something he hadn't caught, something that made his comrades laugh. Something meant to be her answer to his question about the future of Icelandic nationality. He chased after her, fearing his friends had insulted her; he watched her storm along the street, so small but so big; he had longed to speed up, to simply take her in his arms, to run out of town with her, up to the river Elliðaá or something. To fall asleep there in her arms. But she wasn't about to let him catch her; she turned without warning into an alley, and he briskly followed. He grabbed her shoulder. She turned around with a powerful force, as if she knew exactly who was standing behind her. Her face frightened him, thrilled him, so he had to appear cool and serious in his uncontrollable desire to say something romantic—all the words he had thought of for so long. But then she put on this strange face, this strange grimace, and began to giggle. He had seen her scowl like that before, but he didn't understand any more now than he had then how this nonsense could be so graceful and seductive, and he felt all his sublime thoughts shrinking and withering. And he, too, started giggling. It gave him a strange sense of well-being. It was liberating, yet he was anything but free: he was completely in thrall to this strange girl, who was no ordinary bluestocking with inky fingers, but lucid and perceptive by nature. He stepped closer to her, took her bright face in his hands, and kissed her as hard as he could, and when he had done so, he kissed her as gently as he could, longer and longer until some town tramp yelled into the alley, and she broke free and headed inland, home to her little house.

The servant girl, the one and only, had entered the Governor's office just as Jón pulled the purse from the brown parcel. Of course, she was highly interested in the matter of the meeting, so she kept finding things to do while Jón examined the purse. When his observation seemed without end, the Governor broke the silence and asked if he recognize the purse. His answer was far from convincing: "Why would I?" The Governor asked him to check its contents. No young man would feel at ease digging into this woman's purse right here in the office, so he was a little nervous when he tried to loosen the strap that fastened it. He stuck his slender but strong hand inside the purse and dug out a pen stem, a broken hair comb, a tiny, nail-thin notebook marked "Selena Branson," a pencil stub, a filthy handkerchief embroidered with S and B, pages from a detective novel, and four pennies. Just before the Editor emptied the whole bag, the master thanked his servant and signaled she should leave his office.

Jón had now got hold of what was at the bottom of the purse: an object in the shape of a cylinder. It was a roll of money with a red silk thread tied around it. He turned it about and looked questioningly at the Governor, who replied, after a moment's silence: "Fifteen thousand dollars!" The maid patted a pillow, brushed at a seat.

Jón adjusted himself in the chair: "Where has this money come from?"

"From inside the purse. It came to Iceland in this purse labeled 'Selena Branson.'"

"Right."

"Indeed. So don't you think that fact indicates Dr. Finnsson's information was correct, his questions legitimate?"

Jón was evidently a little alarmed: "I think this parcel is chiefly a sign something happened to the purse's owner. Selena?"

"Of course, but the parcel confirms the American director's words, and the case shall be investigated as a theft of cultural property. We have the evidence: the purse was sent to Iceland, and that removes all doubt that its owner, the seller of the object, is an Icelandic woman. *Þjófarót*. The flower is Icelandic."

"That flower grows here, there and everywhere."

The Governor looked at the young man, squirming in his chair, his eyes repeatedly looking away. Then he leaned back in his seat, crossed his arms, and pretended to be steadfast: "I have no choice but to confiscate the money. The dollars will go into the national treasury."

And then the young man suddenly looked into the chief's eyes, his voice questioning but clear and unequivocal: "If this is a payment for the object, shouldn't the Antiquarian Collection get the money?"

The Governor clearly didn't expect this reaction from the Editor, but when he realized the young man's implication, he expressed his response with a wide smile. Then he shrugged his shoulders and turned down his mouth: "What do you suggest? Let's hear you out!"

In the silence which reigned inside the office of the Danish King's highest official in Iceland, the maid could no longer stand there with one eye to the narrow slit between the frame and the door. She gently closed the chink and pushed her ear up to the door panel. Jón could be heard clearing his throat: "As you well know . . ." But before the rest of these words could drift from the room, through the wall and into the girl's ear, someone blew a trumpet! The sound was far away, but loud and unexpected enough that she jerked and lost the thread. With her hand on her chest, cursing softly, she walked to the house's main entrance. She opened the door to Lækjartorg, looking north, toward the sea. Fog on the horizon.

The ship approaches land after a difficult week at sea. Bearing a variety of goods, all sorts of passengers. People band together in groups on the deck; the crew is in fine spirits. Back in the stern, several men clink glasses: the Danish merchant, the Faroese surveyor, the French naval officer, the English chocolatier, the American prospector, the Scottish painter, the Icelandic antiquarian. Under the lifeboat on the port side sits an ample merchant's wife next to two young girls who have sought treatment abroad for respiratory illness and foot problems. None of them can see through the fog—except, perhaps, the passenger without luggage, who has mostly kept to herself during the journey but who now stands firm in the prow, a tattered hat on her head, one red flower sagging toward its broken brim as she looks to the land from outside it. Every now and then, she slaps her hand to her skirt pocket, muttering something down at her collar, but when she sees the mountains rising from the mist and makes out the hard-to-discern jumble of shacks below the rocky slopes and hillock, she suddenly falls still. A dreamy, mysterious image, yet more real than anything else she has ever seen. She thinks of the story she has narrated in her head, about her travels through the wonders and intricacies of a foreign city. With this earth now here before her, she feels the story can hardly be true. Too many ridiculous coincidences. All of it one false pretense after another. A bit like the plot of a penny dreadful.

SIGRÚN PÁLSDÓTTIR completed a PhD in the History of Ideas at the University of Oxford in 2001, after which she was a research fellow at the University of Iceland and the editor of *Saga*, the principal peer-reviewed journal for Icelandic history. She first came to prominence as an author of historical biographies, including the nineteenth-century biography *Thora. A Bishop's Daughter* (2010) and *Uncertain Seas* (2013), a story of a young couple and their three children who were killed when sailing from New York to Iceland aboard a ship torpedoed by a German submarine in 1944. First published as *Kompa* in 2016, her debut novel *History: A Mess* was the first to be translated into English (Open Letter, 2019). Pálsdóttir's work has been nominated for the Icelandic Literary Prize, Icelandic Women's Literature Prize, Hagþenkir Non-fiction Prize, the DV Culture Prize, and Uncertain Seas won The Icelandic Booksellers' Prize in 2013. *Embroidery* is her second novel, and was awarded The European Union Prize for Fiction 2021.

LYTTON SMITH has translated over a dozen novels and nonfiction books from the Icelandic, including works by Andri Snær Magnason, Bragi Ólafsson, Kristín Ómarsdóttir, and Ófeigur Sigurðsson. He was awarded a 2019 Literary Arts Fellowship in Translation from the National Endowment for the Arts. He has published five poetry collections including, most recently, *The Square*, winner of the 2020 NMP/Diagram Chapbook Contest.

CPSIA information can be obtained
at www.ICGtesting.com
Printed in the USA
JSHW020340060423
39983JS00002B/2

9 781948 830768